NOT YOU AGAIN

TERRI OSBURN

Cover 2021 Bookin' It Designs

CHAPTER ONE

FOUR BLIND DATES IN FIVE DAYS. WHY DID I AGREE TO this again?

Oh, right. Because I'm a people pleaser willing to suffer so that my friends will stop worrying about me. A woman my age—four months shy of the big three oh—should not cave to peer pressure, but when the most important women in your life team up against you, resistance is futile. They nag because they care.

They want me to be happy. To move on. What they don't believe is that I *have* moved on, and I shouldn't have to date a man to prove it. Something I've repeated several times yet no one listens, so if going on these meaningless blind dates was what it took to put this subject to rest once and for all, I was willing to do it.

The *five days* part was due to my job. As an event planner, I didn't have much time to socialize since most weekends were spent overseeing a party of some sort. It had taken a Herculean effort but I'd managed to twist my schedule to get this one full week with no active events. I still had the regular meetings during the day, but five consecutive nights without having to be on hand at a single event was nothing short of a miracle.

So here I was, lingering at the northeast corner of Market Square in downtown Pittsburgh, scanning the area for a face I'd seen only once in a low-quality picture the day before. I hadn't thought to ask Josie—one of my best friends since college who set this up—if she'd offered the same courtesy to my date. Spotting someone who looked like the guy in the picture, I crossed the sidewalk in his direction, but another woman approached him first. An affectionate greeting was exchanged, making it clear that I had *not* found the right person.

At least I hoped not.

"Becca Witherspoon?" came a voice from my right.

"That's me," I replied with a spin.

"I'm Peter, the broker," he said. "I'm your date."

Uncertain how these things worked, I extended a hand and said, "I'm Becca the event planner." He'd already said my name so clearly this was redundant, but my mouth had disengaged from my brain. I hadn't expected to be nervous, yet meeting a stranger, even with less-than-genuine intentions, was still stressful.

When he accepted the greeting and leaned in for a

hug, I stiffened in response. After two awkward pats on my back, he stepped away. "Should we go inside then?"

"We should." I waited for him to go first and we ended up staring at each other for several seconds before I realized he was waiting for me to do the same. Catching the hint, I nodded and shuffled off toward the restaurant entrance.

At the hostess stand, he said, "We have a reservation under Laghari for six thirty."

A pretty young woman with a round face and coke-bottle glasses checked her list before looking up with a smile. "Your table is ready. Follow me, please."

She led us through the long narrow dining room to a table on the right in front of a pastoral wall mural of an Italian countryside. Italian was my favorite kind of food so when Josie let me know Peter had picked this location, I'd been relieved to find, if nothing else, I would get an excellent dinner out of this deal. I took the booth side of the table, against the mural-painted wall and Peter sat across from me in a beige chair.

"Have you dined with us before?" the hostess—Justine according to her name tag—asked.

"I have," Peter replied. "Have you, Becca?"

"Yes, I have. This is one of my favorite restaurants."

My date smiled as his shoulders visibly relaxed, and my earlier anxiety fled. He was cute with kind eyes and a tiny dark curl that lingered just above his brow. As always, the comparisons ran through my mind. He lacked

Brian's dimples and cleft chin. His voice wasn't as deep and his shoulders not as broad. But this wasn't about finding another Brian. That would never happen. This was about meeting my friend's colleague for a nice meal and checking one date off the list.

"Great," Justine said. "Albert will be taking care of you this evening and he'll be with you shortly. Until then, can I get you some wine?"

"Pinot grigio for me," Peter replied.

"And you?" she said, turning my way.

Thanks to a hectic day I hadn't eaten in several hours, and one glass of wine would put me under the table. "I'll stick with water, thank you."

"No problem. If you change your mind, just let Albert know."

Justine left us and the awkwardness returned as we perused our menus. "Do you like working in finance?" I asked to break the silence.

Sliding the dark-rimmed glasses up his nose, he nodded. "I do." Taking me by surprise, he countered with, "Have you dated anyone recently?"

"No," I replied, wishing I'd kept my mouth shut. "You?"

"I have." I wasn't sure what to do with this information and embraced my right to remain silent.

"So you're an event planner?" he asked.

I rolled with the topic change. "I am. It's our busy

season with June around the corner and life has been a bit crazy."

A tall man in a white shirt and black pants stepped up to the table. "Good evening, folks. I'm Albert and I'll be your server tonight." After filling my glass, he set a small carafe of water on the table and proceeded to fill Peter's wineglass from a bottle he'd had tucked under his arm. "Justine let me know that you've both dined with us before so I'm guessing you're acquainted with the menu, but just in case, do you have any questions?"

"I don't," I replied, then checked with my date. "Do you?"

Peter swallowed his entire glass of wine before responding. "I'm good, but I'd like a martini. Dirty, with gin not vodka."

Albert accepted the empty wineglass with an unreadable expression, and I hoped mine was the same. I had no problem with anyone drinking alcohol, but the speed with which he'd downed the wine concerned me. Peter carried a tension that went beyond the nerves of a blind date.

"A martini it is. Are you ready to order your meals?"

"I'm ready," I said, eager to move things along. "I'd like the Pappardelle Bolognese, please."

"Pork, beef, or veal?" the waiter asked.

"Beef, thank you."

"That's what Evelyn always ordered," Peter murmured.

"Who is Evelyn?" I asked.

"No one. I'll have the Caramelle."

"Yes, sir. I'll get your orders in and be right back with that martini."

"Why is June your busy season?" Peter asked as Albert walked away and I was still wondering about Evelyn.

"June is a big month for weddings," I explained. "That means a lot of last-minute details have to be worked out this month."

"Have you ever been married?"

My chest tightened as I gave the short answer. "No."

"Why not?"

"No particular reason," I lied. Time to change the subject. "Are you originally from Pittsburgh?"

"No, I grew up in Silver Spring, Maryland. I went to Pitt and decided to stay after graduation. Do you want to get married?"

Unprepared for the question, I took a sip of water before responding. "Is that a proposal?" I joked. I knew full well what he'd meant. I just didn't want to answer.

"Of course not. We just met."

This was going from bad to worse.

"Yes, I know. I was kidding."

"Oh." Peter didn't crack a smile and after an extended silence, Albert thankfully returned as promised.

"Your food should be out shortly," he said as Peter reached for the martini before the glass touched the table.

"Thank you," I said with a smile, then watched Peter

attack the foggy drink like a dying man and down most of it in one swallow.

Thirst seemingly quenched, he said, "I almost proposed once." His eyes remained locked on the glass and I wondered if he'd meant to say the thought aloud. After finishing off the rest of the drink, he said, "Where did you grow up?"

There was something going on here that had nothing to do with me or this date.

"I'm born and raised in the area," I replied, reaching for my water. "My family has lived in Carnegie for generations."

"I'm surprised you don't have a stronger accent then."

A fair statement. Most locals sounded like someone loaded the Boston and New York accents into a blender and added a hefty dose of yinz to the mix. The only reason I *didn't* sound like the rest of my relatives was my occupation—convincing potential customers to trust you with thousands of dollars went better with a more professional accent.

"I can turn it on when I want to," I assured him.

The food arrived and as Albert set the plates on the table, Peter held up his empty glass. "I'll take another one of these," he said.

Between the drinking and the random mentions of another woman, I recognized the situation I was in. Peter and I had a few things in common but his wound was clearly fresher than mine. Not a dream date scenario, but since I hadn't walked into this situation with the best of intentions, the least I could do was offer a sympathetic ear.

Albert walked away with yet another empty glass, and I said, "Would you like to talk about Evelyn?"

Peter's brown eyes went wide behind the dark frames. "How do you know about Evelyn?"

The poor guy had no idea. "You said her name earlier. I don't mind listening if you want to talk about it."

His eyes shifted from his food to the mural behind me before he said, "She's someone I work with."

So he had to see her all the time. "Was she more than a coworker at some point?"

The curt nod spoke volumes.

"That's never an easy situation." I'd never dated a coworker but forced proximity with an ex must have been difficult.

"We dated for a year until three weeks ago when I found out that she was *also* dating Roger Mertens. Not that I care." The speed with which he was downing martinis said he very much cared. "If she wants to date the biggest snitch in Human Resources," he added, his fork swinging dangerously, "then she never deserved me."

Wanting to support this statement, I said, "I agree."

"I can do better," he muttered.

I would have been flattered but this was said without even a glance in my direction.

"How are we doing?" Albert asked as he set the new martini on the table. "Can I get you anything?"

"We're good, thank you," I said.

The waiter strolled off as I kept my eyes on my plate. Lending a sympathetic ear was one thing. Becoming an accessory to the headache Peter would have tomorrow was another.

"I don't normally drink on a weeknight," he said, drawing my attention. When I looked up, he added, "I'm not going to get drunk or anything. It's just been *a week*."

I agreed. And it was only Tuesday.

Forty minutes later, Peter the Broker made a liar out of himself by getting thoroughly drunk. Possibly closer to shit-faced, as Aunt Jeanne called it when Uncle Reginald had enough Iron City beers to piss his own pants. Hopefully, this date would not include Peter wetting himself. I'd assumed we would go Dutch on the meal, but by the time the check came, my heartbroken date could hardly sit upright let alone whip out a credit card, so I paid in full. Josie would be getting a bill for his half.

He'd ordered two more dirty martinis and barely touched his food. Partly because he'd been too busy talking about Evelyn. Apparently, the month before her infidelity had come to light, they'd shopped around for an apartment, and Peter had put a down payment on a sizable ring. He showed me a picture of it on his phone and the man had excellent taste. In my line of work, I'd seen every ring out there and Evelyn had cheated herself out of a beautiful setting.

To make matters worse, the cheating had been revealed through an email between coworkers that he'd been mistakenly cc'd on. The more I learned, the more I had to agree that Peter absolutely had grounds for tying one on. I'd have preferred he not do so while on a date with me, but who was I to judge? I'd swallowed my fair share of alcohol two years ago when my heart got broken.

Once the check was paid, Albert helped me get my date outside where I then had to figure out how to get him home. He was in no condition to drive, and I didn't have a license. Did I put him in a car and hope he made it home? That didn't feel right. In his current condition, he might pass out on the way and who knew where the driver would leave him. I'd have to go along, and then get myself home.

"I need you to focus," I pleaded, cupping Peter's face in my hands. "Where do you live?"

I pulled up my trusty app, prepared to enter his address but, of course, he couldn't make it that easy.

"In my apartment."

Jaw tight, I tried again. "Where would that be?"

"Are you trying to come home with me?" he asked with half-closed eyes and a lopsided grin.

"No," I assured him. "But since you're in no condition to drive, we'll have to order a car."

"But I have a car."

I'd handled enough drunk wedding guests over the years to have a degree in this sort of thing, but in those cases said guests had ultimately been someone else's problem. This one was mine alone, and I was quickly running out of patience. Lucky for him that I wasn't heartless enough to abandon him in the middle of Market Square.

"You obviously can't drive in your condition," I explained, "so I need your address to put in the app. Where do you live?"

"The South Side," he replied. It was a start, but not nearly the details I needed.

"Where, exactly?" I pressed.

Glasses perched on the end of his nose, he attempted to focus on my face. "Sidney Street. Twenty-nine fifteen Sidney Street."

Finally. I entered the address into my phone and the first option—a car two blocks away—popped up. "We're all set," I said, confirming the ride with a quick touch of the screen. "Jacob to the rescue."

"Who is Jacob?"

"Our driver."

"Is he driving my car?"

"You'll have to get your car tomorrow." Following the instructions on the phone, I took Peter's hand. "He's going to pick us up down this way."

To my surprise, my date spun me in a circle and said, "You aren't as pretty as Evelyn, but I like you."

The move threw us both off-balance, sending me toppling into a passing couple and Peter onto his butt on the sidewalk. A pigeon squawked in protest before whooshing past my head, and after a sincere apology to the passersby, I attempted to lift my dance partner to his feet. For a man who looked as if he'd need to run around in the shower to get wet, he was quite heavy.

During the struggle, a white Buick pulled up to the curb. The passenger window slid down and a voice said, "Meredith?"

My mother had blessed me with the name Meredith, after her own mother, but to avoid confusion, the family had used my middle name Rebecca. That had been shortened to Becca by middle school. However, anything tied to a credit card was easier if I used my first name. A detail the drivers who shuttled me around the city had no need to know.

"Yes, that's me," I replied. "Are you Jacob?" Normally, I would check the license plate to make sure I was climbing into the correct vehicle, but none of this was normal.

"I am." The window went back up, and I spun to see Peter still on the ground.

"You have to stand up." I tried lifting him from behind with no luck, then I switched to pulling from the front, but he still didn't budge. At five foot two and barely one hundred pounds, I'd never been much of a power lifter. "Come on, Peter. Help me out here."

As the challenge continued, the passenger window slid down again. “Are you getting in?”

Frustrated, I huffed the hair out of my face and said, “I can’t get him up.” That sounded far less dirty in my head.

Dark brows arched my way as an awkward silence passed. I feared he might drive off, but instead, he opened his door and climbed out. I hadn’t been able to see him well inside the car, but when he joined me on the sidewalk, my breath caught. At well over six feet, the man carried himself like one of those action heroes who never gets rattled.

The ones who have all the best lines, carried the perfect amount of scruff along their chiseled jawline, and morphed into a total badass when necessary. He also looked as if he’d walked right out of one of the Asian dramas I’d devoured on my rare nights off. The cheekbones alone could make a girl swoon.

“Time to get up, buddy.” Jacob the Driver lifted Peter the Broker as if he weighed no more than a sack of groceries. Before I could recover, my date was safely in the back seat. “Your turn,” the driver said, glancing my way.

I emitted some sort of giggle slash snort combination before shuffling in beside Peter, trying not to suffocate on my embarrassment.

Jacob closed the door and seconds later was back in the driver’s seat. The local rock station played on the radio, the volume just high enough to prevent total silence as the Buick cut through the early evening traffic with ease. Suddenly exhausted, I closed my eyes and thought about all the ways I was going to make Josie pay for this. Covering Peter's half of dinner would be only the beginning.

CHAPTER TWO

OUR DRIVER SEEMED TO KNOW EXACTLY WHERE TO TURN to avoid both the daring pedestrians and the massive city buses that rarely yielded to other vehicles. As we rode in silence, I caught glimpses of him in the rearview mirror. He had a pleasant face, short dark hair, and full lips with a perfect bow shape along the top. Though he wasn't smiling, he wasn't scowling either, and I had the inexplicable feeling that I was in good hands. That I was safe.

Not that Pittsburgh was all that dangerous or that I feared other drivers. I was simply a person who never truly relaxed. It wasn't in my nature. Yet as we sailed through the city streets, I felt lighter. As if the man in the front seat had everything under control, and for the next few minutes at least, I didn't have to think about anything.

"Thank you," I said, grateful once again that he

hadn't abandoned the ride. "I didn't realize he would be that heavy."

"No problem," he replied, meeting my gaze in the mirror.

When our eyes met, a tingle swept up my spine. His gaze returned to the road and I gave myself a mental shake. What the heck was I doing? I was no better than Evelyn at this point. Not that I would be seeing Peter the Broker again, but I should at least refrain from picking up a new man while still on a date with him.

A laughable thought. I'd never picked up a man in my life, literally—obviously—or figuratively speaking. Brian and I had been high school sweethearts and I hadn't dated since he'd… left.

The Buick made a quick right off Boulevard of the Allies onto Second Avenue, tossing Peter against my side. "Are we going home?" he asked.

"We are," I replied.

"Did we have a good time?"

Doubtful he'd remember this conversation, I lied. "Loads."

"I'm glad," he said, dropping his head onto my shoulder.

"That makes one of us," I muttered and caught Jacob's gaze in the mirror.

His expression changed and the disapproval hit like a smack. Bristling, I told myself to ignore him. Why should I care what a stranger I'd never see again thought of me?

I was the one who'd endured an hour of listening to Peter whine about his ex-girlfriend and her tattletale lover. And I was the one whose neck he was currently breathing on.

With a gentle nudge, I sent my cohort back to his side of the car.

The trip up Second Avenue seemed to take forever and Peter's head landed on my shoulder three more times. Thankfully, he wasn't sober enough to try anything serious, and I did feel bad when I nudged him again and his head bounced off the car door window. This was his own fault though. I could have left him to fend for himself. Okay, I'd never do that, but someone else might have.

As we turned right onto the Hot Metal Bridge, Peter's head smacked off the glass again.

Leaning over him, I positioned my purse as a pillow. "Lay on this."

He settled against the soft pink leather with a sigh and a smile, his mind seemingly free of Evelyn, at least for now. At the end of the bridge, Jacob made a left and turned into the parking lot of a large apartment building that looked to have been a factory in a former life.

"Here you go," he announced.

I tapped Peter. "We're here." His eyes remained closed. "Peter? Are you awake?"

"Uh-huh."

Why hadn't I gotten coffee into him before ordering the car?

"You need to get out now." Eyes still closed, he patted

around for the door handle but found his own knee instead. I tossed the purse onto the seat beside me and reached across him. "I'll get it."

The door flew open and we both tumbled out. When Peter's head hit the pavement, he grunted in pain, while his foot kicked me in the boob. My yelp was followed by a few choice words as I teetered between agony and humiliation. Half in the car and half out, I struggled to right myself, and when I finally reached a sitting position, I looked up to find our driver looming above us both.

"Can you get him inside?" he asked.

Knowing my limitations, I said, "Probably not, but I'm hoping he can walk."

The driver scratched his head. "How much did he drink?"

"One glass of wine and four martinis." I stood up, careful not to step on my date. "He told me he wasn't going to get drunk."

Squatting, he tapped Peter on the cheek. "He lied. Time to get up, buddy. Help your girlfriend out and get to your feet."

"I'm not his girlfriend," I corrected.

Brow arched, he looked up at me. "Does he know that?"

As if to answer for me, Peter said, "I love Evelyn."

"See?" I replied. "He loves Evelyn."

Jacob shook his head. "Then can Evelyn help get him out from under my car?"

I hadn't noticed that Peter's feet were under the vehicle. If Jacob tried to pull away, he'd have to run over my date to do it.

Kneeling down, I tapped Peter's cheek as Jacob had, only harder. "Come on. You have to wake up." Tap, tap, tap. "Peter, wake up."

Bushy brows furrowed. "Let me sleep a little longer."

"On your feet," Jacob said, lifting the drunk man first to a sitting position, and then upright. "Steady now." He slowly eased his hands away, allowing Peter to stand on his own. To me he said, "He's all yours."

"Thank you again." I wedged myself under Peter's right arm and moved us both out of the way so the beleaguered driver, who had already shown more patience than this situation deserved, could close the car door.

Four steps later, my cargo nearly collapsed. I managed to keep us upright, though I had no idea how. Our progress was slow, and I realized there were no doors in sight, nor did I see signs leading to an entrance. I also had no idea how to find Peter's apartment. As I was about to ask for his apartment number, my load got lighter.

"Wha—"

"Which way is it?" Jacob asked, shifting my useless date's weight onto himself.

The man was too nice for his own good, and he definitely wasn't going to like my answer.

"I don't know."

Brown eyes turned my way, and I was struck by the

length of his eyelashes. He probably wouldn't appreciate being called pretty, but that was the exact word that came to mind. Actually, he veered closer to beautiful.

"You don't know?"

There was that judgmental glare again. "I just met him less than two hours ago."

"Do you make a habit of picking up drunk men in bars and taking them home?"

I could hardly unpack all of the accusations in that statement.

"Not that I owe you any sort of explanation, but no, I do not. We were on a blind date, and he was sober when I met him. I had no idea he would get like this. If anything, you should be impressed that I'm going to such lengths to get a virtual stranger home safely."

"You want credit when I'm the one carrying him?"

Touché.

"A mere technicality." Arguing was getting us nowhere so I turned my attention to the source of my problem. "Peter, wake up. We need your apartment number."

"Three oh four," he replied.

Jacob and I locked eyes, both surprised by the quick reply.

"You're awake?" I said, pointing out the obvious.

"Who could sleep with you two making so much noise?"

Eyes half open, Peter stepped away from Jacob,

surveyed his surroundings, and then strolled down the sidewalk to our left. He swayed a bit but remained upright and continued on at a steady pace.

When he disappeared around the corner of the building I looked up at Jacob. "What if he falls again?"

Heading back to his car, he said, "He'll be fine."

He was probably right. And if Peter didn't make it all the way to his own door, surely a neighbor would find him sleeping it off somewhere in the building. Declaring the disaster of a date officially over, I spun toward my ride, only to find the Buick backing out of the parking space.

"Hey! Wait for me."

Whether he hadn't heard or was purposely ignoring me I didn't know, but Jacob drove out of the parking lot, leaving me once again in need of a ride. Now I had to order another car. With a sigh, I reached for my purse, but it wasn't on my hip where it should have been.

"Oh no." I patted myself down as if the pink Longchamps bag I'd bought in Paris might be tucked inside a secret pocket. Damn it, that was my favorite purse. And double damn, my phone was in it.

By some miracle, the white Buick was still sitting at the traffic light, and I broke into a run across the parking lot. I was thirty feet from reaching him when the light turned green, and I started screaming like a crazy woman.

"Jacob! Wait! *Wait*!"

Arms flailing, I changed direction so he would see me

as he rounded the corner. With my eyes locked on the moving car, I failed to spot the low-hanging branch before it smacked me in the forehead, sending me to the ground.

"Ow, ow, ow." Hands on my head, I stayed on my back. "Could this get any freaking worse?" I asked no one in particular.

"Are you always this much trouble?" a deep voice asked.

Eyes shut tight, I sighed. I was too tired and humiliated to offer a witty comeback. "My phone and purse are in your car."

Several seconds passed before he spoke again. "Are you going to get up?"

"Give me a second. I was just attacked by an oak."

"It's a sycamore," he corrected. Heartless. The man was absolutely heartless. "How are you getting home?"

I removed the hand from my forehead and checked for blood. Thankfully, it was clean.

"I was going to order another car, but you had my phone."

He extended a hand. "Come on. I'll take you."

Desperate for this night to end, I slid my hand into his, which was strong and clean and twice the size of mine. Once upright, I straightened my clothes and brushed off my skirt, then retrieved the flat that had come off during my fall. The tree had literally knocked me out of my shoe.

"How does it look?" I asked, tilting my face up for his examination.

A warm thumb gently brushed my bangs aside. "You're going to have an ugly bruise, but it didn't break the skin."

I shook my hair back into place, bringing on a sudden bout of vertigo.

"Whoa," Jacob mumbled, his hands on my upper arms. "You good?"

Blinking, I waited for the dizziness to pass before looking up again. Full lips curved down with concern as he watched me closely. I nearly reached out to touch them.

"I need to go home."

"Where do you live?" he asked.

"Two hundred Cowan Street in the old Prospect School building."

With a half smile that took my breath away, he nodded. "Okay then. Let's go."

I'd have gone anywhere with him in that moment, but that euphoric feeling did not last long.

"You shouldn't sleep for a while," Jacob said, interrupting my nap.

"Why not?"

"You just took a hit to the head."

He had a point. "Yes, I did. And I have the headache to show for it."

Jacob checked under my bangs again. "You'll need to ice it. Is there someone at your place to keep an eye on you?"

"Just Milo," I replied, "but I doubt he'll be much help."

"Why not?"

"You know how they are."

"Men?" he asked.

"Cats, but men aren't at the top of my list right now either."

Whether he was offended or caught the hint I didn't know, but Jacob went quiet after that. Thankfully, the South Side wasn't far from Mount Washington, where I lived.

He was right about the head injury, so I sat up straighter and stared out the passenger window. At Peter's apartment building, I'd tried to climb into the back seat, but since Jacob was providing this ride out of the goodness of his heart and not through the app, he'd insisted that I sit in the front. Something about not being a chauffeur when he didn't have to be.

I watched a standard poodle drag its owner down the sidewalk as a young boy darted around them, pirate's hat pulled low over his eyes and a grin on his face. Window after window sported Penguin signs. The regular hockey season had ended back in April, but the Pens were in the playoffs again, so the buzz continued into May. Pittsburgh had been a hockey town since I was an infant, when Dad and Uncle Reginald had been proud season ticket holders. My brother Joey and our cousin Tony had the seats now. I served as Joey's backup when he couldn't make a game, but he rarely missed, especially during the playoffs.

Jacob took a left and the view changed. Trees showing off their new leaves filled the landscape. I'd heard many complaints over the years that Pittsburgh was nothing but gray, but there was plenty of greenery if you knew where to look. At least at certain times of the year, and May was one of them.

My eyes grew heavy again, and not solely from the headache. This was my busiest time of year, and I'd stayed up way too late the night before going over the plan for the Matheson event. The bride and her mother had been my last meeting of the day before my date, and though I prided myself on never missing a detail, these particular clients were more meticulous than most, which added more stress to my plate.

"You awake over there?" Jacob said, startling me.

Lifting my head from the passenger door and having no idea how it got there, I said, "I am now."

"Somebody other than Milo needs to keep an eye on you for the next couple of hours."

He had a point and I knew just the person. "A friend of mine lives in my building. I'll have her come down to my apartment." Pulling up Josie's number in my phone, I added, "I need to have a word with her anyway."

I'd planned to go home and go to bed, purposely making her suffer until tomorrow to hear how things went, but I also preferred not to die in my sleep. I fired off the text to meet me at my place in twenty minutes and dropped the phone back into my lap.

"Thank you for your help tonight," I said. "I'd probably still be trying to get Peter home if it weren't for you."

"You're welcome."

"I bet you see all sorts of things in this job."

"Yep," he replied, navigating the car around a slow-moving minivan.

I needed to feel better about this cluster of an evening, so I pushed for a better answer.

"Dates that went way worse than this one, right?"

Dark eyes cut my way for half a second before he shook his head. "I wouldn't say that."

The thumping in my head increased. "That can't be true," I argued.

Brow furrowed, he said, "The guy drunk off his feet by eight. The woman almost taken out by a branch. That's tough to beat."

If there'd been a hint of a smile, I'd have said he was teasing, but I was starting to believe the man never smiled. Except for that grin that had lured me into this free ride.

"The branch was your fault. If you hadn't tried to leave me, then I wouldn't have had to chase you down."

"You never said you needed a ride."

I spun to face him. "I told you that I'd just met him and that I didn't even know where his apartment was. I clearly didn't drive myself there, so how did you think I was going to get home?"

"You didn't put a second stop in the app," he defended. "I picked up and delivered to the address I was given. The ride was over."

Damn it, he was right again. If I hadn't been so busy trying to keep Peter upright, I would have taken the time to enter both of our addresses. But still. He'd nearly left me stranded.

"You could have at least *asked* if I had a way home," I said, sounding whinier than intended. The headache was getting worse, making it difficult to keep my inner four-year-old contained. "What would have happened if I hadn't caught you? I had no phone to even call a friend."

That grin returned. "Technically, you didn't catch me."

"You are not cute," I growled, making the pain worse. "That's my building ahead. You can make the right on Norton and pull into the back parking lot. That'll put me closer to my apartment." He did as asked without comment. "It's the door straight ahead," I directed.

"Yes, ma'am," he said, unaffected by my obvious agitation.

I pulled my keys from my purse. “Thank you.”

As I climbed out, he said, “Hey.” I glanced back to discover a look of mild concern in his dark eyes. “Don’t forget to ice it.”

How was I supposed to dislike him when he kept being nice like that?

“I won’t.”

I crossed the short distance to the building, not realizing until I’d pulled the heavy door open that the Buick hadn’t moved. I turned back and gave a wave, receiving a head nod of acknowledgment in return before the car drove off.

Lingering inside the door, I pulled up the app and left a hefty tip, as well as a five-star rating. Despite my annoyance, Jacob had more than earned both, and now maybe he wouldn’t tell his friends about the klutzy woman and her drunk date who’d provided his Tuesday evening entertainment. As I made my way up the stairs to the second floor, my legs felt heavy and my back started to ache. Flexing, I felt a twinge of pain in my right shoulder blade.

“Stupid tree,” I muttered, realizing I was going to have more than just the bruise on my head to show for this night. At least the first date was done. Three more to go and I had to believe the rest would go better than this one. I wasn’t looking for a love connection, but surviving the week without any further contusions didn’t seem like too much to ask.

CHAPTER THREE

"JESUS, BECCA, WHAT DID THAT JAGOFF DO TO YOU?"

Josie Danvers—my upstairs neighbor, friend since college, and the person responsible for my date from hell—slammed the door behind her, and a jolt of pain shot through my temples.

"Not so loud." I held the makeshift ice pack to my forehead. "This isn't Peter's fault. I ran into a tree."

"A tree?" she said, following me into the living room. "That doesn't even make sense."

No, it didn't. I stopped before the sofa and checked the throbbing forehead bump in the giant round mirror on the wall, which I'd found at a yard sale the month before. A total steal at ten dollars. The tender skin was quickly turning purple, and the ice was doing little to take down the swelling.

"Why did you set me up with a man who's in love with someone else?" I asked, taking a seat on the couch and curling my legs beneath me. Milo hopped up onto the back of the couch and stretched out beside my shoulder.

Josie took the other end and hugged my latest flea market find—an apricot-colored pillow—to her chest. Her blond hair was pulled up in a high ponytail that made her look twelve, while heavy, dark-rimmed glasses gave her a brainy hipster look. She would never be caught dead wearing the glasses in public. That's what contacts were for.

"He's in love with Evelyn? I thought they were just fuck buddies."

"You thought wrong."

She leaned forward to examine my injury. "I'm sorry, Becks." Josie had been calling me that since we'd met freshman year of college. "I thought if he found the perfect girl he'd forget about Evelyn."

"What made you think I was the perfect girl for Peter the Broker?"

"Peter the Broker?" she repeated.

"That's how he introduced himself," I explained, absently rubbing Milo's chin. He purred in feline bliss.

Josie nodded. "Makes sense. I picked him for two reasons. First, you're everything Evelyn is not. Kind. Caring. Laid-back. And this has nothing to do with anything, but she's got this long dark hair that used to be blond, but she's letting it grow out so the bottom four inches are still platinum. I have no idea why she doesn't cut it off or color it to match the rest, and I don't like her enough to ask."

"Why don't you like her?"

Josie narrowed her eyes and cut her gaze to the ceiling. "She has this air about her like she thinks she's better than the rest of us. She only goes to lunch with the guys, and personally, I think she likes the attention. Come to think of it, I'm not sure she has any female friends at work."

"Have you ever talked to her?" I asked.

"Barely. Small talk in the bathroom once."

I pointed out the obvious. "Then you don't really know her. Maybe she's shy or insecure. Maybe she thinks you all hate her so she puts on airs to cover the hurt."

Shoulders dropping, Josie leaned her head on the back of the couch. "You think so?"

"I do. Peter didn't seem like the kind of guy who would get hung up on the woman you're describing." Not that he was feeling all that positive about Evelyn at the moment, but he must have seen something good to want to marry her.

"I'll feel really bad if that's the case."

I had a hunch it was. "Invite her to lunch. It sounds like she could use a friend."

Josie stayed quiet for several seconds as the possibilities settled in her mind. We'd been through this junior year when Megan Knox—another member of our small circle—had become my roommate. Megan and I had met in a marketing class sophomore year and if she hadn't found a roommate for the next semester, she'd have been forced to drop out and move back home. Her family weren't firm believers in education and saw her insistence on getting a degree as a waste of money.

Josie had gone with her first impression of Megan, which had been bumpy at best. A city girl through and through, she'd scared Megan half to death with her direct stare and boundless confidence. There was a reason that Josie had gone into finance while Megan became a librarian. Thankfully, the pair had learned to get along and nearly ten years later, Josie would fight anyone who messed with her quiet and sensitive friend.

"Anyway," Josie continued, "Evelyn is the third woman Peter has dated at the firm and all have ended in disaster."

"Did they all cheat on him?"

"Cheat?" Josie's brown eyes went wide. "Evelyn cheated on him?"

"According to Peter, she did. He kept talking about her dating some snitch from HR."

Bouncing onto her knees, she hugged the pillow tighter and got an evil look from Milo, who'd been jostled on his perch. "Evelyn is seeing Roger Mertens? No fucking way. That dude is a total narc."

I had not invited her here to have a gossip session. "Could you take a little less pleasure in this story? Peter is so heartbroken that he got thoroughly trashed by the time the waiter cleared our plates, and I had to get him home. Which wasn't easy. Now I have a grass stain on my pink tweed skirt and what looks like a dirty baseball growing out of my forehead."

Her fingertip brushed the bruise and I winced. "I really am sorry. I also picked him because he's a fun guy and I thought you could use a little more fun in your life. I'd never have set this up if I'd known how badly it would go. Maybe the guy Donna picked will be better."

I hoped so. My friends believed I'd agreed to these dates because I legitimately wanted to find a man. Surely they'd put *some* thought into who they were fixing me up with. Even if Peter hadn't been nursing a broken heart, he hadn't seemed like my type. Not that I knew exactly what my type might be. My only dating experience had been with one person, and he'd been the love of my life. What were the chances of having two loves like that? Not very high.

Thanks to our respective jobs—mine as an event planner and Donna's as a wedding photographer—the two of us spent a lot of time together. That meant she *should* have a reasonable insight into what kind of guy I might like. Sadly, based solely on the little I'd heard about her choice, I had to wonder what she was thinking.

"I'm not sure about that."

"What has she told you about him?" Josie asked.

"Not much." Since I wasn't going out with any of these guys to actually make a connection, I made the mistake of not asking a lot of questions during the setup process. "He's her neighbor, a fitness trainer, and supposedly hot." Three qualities that would never even make my list should I actually go looking for a new life partner.

For one, no matter how this went, him living in Donna's building meant there was a high chance for a future encounter. Likely an awkward one since no matter what happened I would not be seeking a second date. Two, I was one of those women who owned a drawer full of yoga pants yet had never actually partaken in the activity. Or any other that required physical exertion for that matter.

Lastly, the hot thing simply meant he was most likely out of my league. Not to say that my former fiancé wasn't attractive. To me he was beautiful, inside and out. But Brian fell more into the nerdy, sweet, lanky category. He'd also have preferred a root canal with no anesthetic over doing any type of exercise.

As for me, I was cute in the *she looks like she's still in high school* way, but I would never fall into the hot category.

Josie uncurled off the couch and strolled into the kitchen. "That sounds promising," she said, snagging a can of pop from the fridge. "What's his name?"

"Adam."

"Very first man of him."

"I'm hoping he's more evolved than that. Can you do me a favor?" I held up the wet tea towel. "My ice melted."

"Of course."

Once she retrieved the towel and returned to the kitchen, I leaned my head against Milo to rest my eyes. What could have been seconds or minutes later, she shook me awake.

"You aren't supposed to go to sleep when you have a head injury," she informed me.

I'd already received this warning once.

"That's the other reason I called you down here. I need someone to keep me awake."

"Oh, right." With pursed lips, she glanced around my tiny living room. "How about a game of rummy?"

The child of a card-loving family, Josie coerced the rest of us into playing at every opportunity. Her years of experience meant she beat us more times than not, which drove Donna and Megan crazy. I lacked the competitive gene and didn't mind losing. All that mattered tonight was that the game would keep me from dying in my sleep. She grabbed the cards from the kitchen drawer, and we relocated to the floor so we would have space to play.

Halfway through the first hand, Josie said, "I really am sorry. I thought you and Peter would make a good pair. But don't worry," she continued, "we'll find your Mr. Right yet."

I'd already found my Mr. Right. His leaving didn't change that. Unfortunately, my friends turned into angry fairy godmothers when I said things like that so I kept the thought to myself and pointed to my forehead. "Or you'll kill me trying."

Probably not smart to tempt fate, but after this dismal first date, I couldn't imagine the rest being any worse.

"You're making me feel bad," she whined, snagging an ace off the pile and setting down a six-card run. "How *did* you run into a tree anyway?"

"I was trying to catch the driver who took us to Peter's place." I shifted so Milo could curl up in my lap. "He had my purse and phone in his car, and I was too busy screaming like a crazy woman to see the branch in time to duck."

Josie cringed. "That sounds painful." A second later, she said, "Wait. You sent me a text from your phone. Does that mean you caught him?"

Drawing a card off the deck, I laid down my three twos. As always, she was going to cream me in this game. "Not exactly. He saw me hit the tree and came back to see if I was okay."

"That was nice of him."

It *was* nice of him. And though I'd found him annoying during the drive home, sparring with him had been kind of fun. If I ever did decide to try the dating thing again, that would be something I'd look for. Brian and I had spent hours having random debates about everything and nothing, and I missed those impassioned conversations.

"Yeah, he was a nice guy," I agreed. And gorgeous. And strong. And if I ignored the judgy bits, he was charming in his own way. Good thing he'd been the driver and not the date or I might have had to rethink my *not taking these seriously* stance.

"I'm out," Josie said, snapping the rest of her hand onto the rug while discarding a jack.

"Shocker," I said and lifted the ice pack back to my head while she gathered the cards together. "The rest of the week can only get better, right?"

Shuffling the deck like a pro in Vegas, she nodded. "Absolutely. This was just one bad night."

I hoped she was right.

THE NEXT MORNING on my walk to the office—an older building five blocks from my apartment and the reason I lived on Mount Washington—I received a text from Donna saying the DeStefano's engagement pictures were ready for review. I sent a reply that I'd stop by in the afternoon, though I'd have to check my calendar for an exact time once I got to my desk. This was the perfect opportunity to press for more details about the next date. This time I would be more prepared.

"What the hell happened to you?" my boss asked as I entered the office.

Amanda Crawford was blunt like that. At forty-eight years old, she'd dedicated the last twenty years of her life to building Three Rivers Events into a small but successful party planning company. She never married or had children, though one late night after a particularly harrowing wedding reception, she'd downed a bottle of wine and mentioned a former fiancé. When I'd asked about him the next day, she claimed to have no idea what I was talking about.

To clients, she was kindness incarnate—an approach she'd adopted out of necessity. Amanda was a large woman. Not obese, but rather she looked as if she could snap a person in two with her bare hands. At just over six feet tall, she towered above the average human and, as if that wasn't enough, she'd been cursed with a terrible case of resting bitch face.

We'd worked together for the last eight years yet she knew little about my life and I knew nothing about hers. Did she have a hobby? Did she read books? Did she like long walks on the beach at sunset?

I had no idea.

"A sycamore tree," I replied.

I dropped my purse and trench coat onto my desk and carried my *City of Champions* coffee mug to the kitchenette in the corner. After three rounds of gin rummy and another two hours of Josie scaring me awake every fifteen minutes, I'd need at least three cups of caffeine before my brain kicked into gear.

On the plus side, I didn't die.

"How was the meeting with the DeStefanos?" she asked, not the least bit interested in how a sycamore had caused my contusion. "Did you convince them to cancel the ice sculpture?"

"I'm afraid not." The single cup brewer sputtered to life as I leaned my hip on the counter to wait. "I did get them to switch from a luge to a standard design."

"Thank God. Those things are so unsanitary. Send the design order to Samuel to make sure we're on his schedule."

Here's where I had to give the bad news. "Unfortunately, the bride and groom are not in agreement as to what the new design should be. She wants a giant ice bouquet to match her own, and he wants the Steelers logo."

Amanda looked up from her computer screen. "Seriously?"

"I'm sure she'll convince him the flowers are the way to go." Or call off the wedding entirely. The couple had fought throughout every meeting we'd had so far. I was used to soon-to-be newlyweds having disagreements before the nuptials, but in cases like the DeStefanos, I had to wonder why they were marrying at all. "How are things coming along with the Jankowski anniversary party?"

"About that." Amanda slid her reading glasses onto the top of her head. "I need you to handle the meeting tomorrow."

Not what I wanted to hear. "I'm not sure I'll have time. Can you move it to fit your schedule?"

Tossing the glasses onto her desk, she rolled her chair back and crossed her arms. "I have something to tell you."

Certain I wasn't going to like what came next, I said, "Let me get my coffee first." The last of the dark liquid flowed into the mug and I dumped in enough powdered creamer to change the color from black to light brown. Returning to my desk, I sat down and said, "Okay, now I'm ready."

I assumed she was about to tell me that we were taking on a new client who needed a wedding planned in a month. We preferred a year and rarely signed on less than six months out.

"I have cancer," she said.

Stunned speechless, a million questions ran through my brain. The only one I managed to pin down was, "Are you serious?" Not my proudest or most sensitive moment. Quickly regrouping, I added, "I mean, are you okay?"

Again, not the best response, but what the hell was a *right* response to such an announcement?

"I start chemo on Friday," she replied, ignoring both of my missteps. "We're going with an aggressive treatment plan, so I'll need you to take on the brunt of the work for the next couple of months. Maybe longer."

My first thought was *how*? I already had a full slate of clients I was struggling to keep up with. Taking on any more would require cloning myself. At the same time, I owed her. When my life fell apart two years ago, Amanda had given me all the time I'd needed to recover, no questions asked. The woman had cancer, for heaven's sake. I couldn't exactly tell her to find someone else. Not that there *was* anyone else. Other than Marquette, who worked part-time as our administrative assistant, we were a two-woman team.

"Of course," I said. "I'll do whatever you need. How long have you—"

"That's settled then," she said, cutting me off and turning once again to her computer.

I stared at my own dark monitor, unsure what had just happened. Did my boss really just tell me that she has cancer and then refused to share a single detail more?

What kind of cancer? How far progressed was it? Was there going to be a surgery and what was the prognosis?

I considered airing these queries but the look on her face, along with the sudden chill coming from her side of the room, kept me quiet. I hoped she at least had someone to go through this with her. As far as I knew, Amanda had no family other than two cousins she couldn't stand, and a grandfather who lived in a home near Harrisburg. She never talked about spending time with friends, nor had she ever brought a visitor into the office.

The last thing she'd want was my pity so I followed her lead and pretended the giant cancer elephant wasn't hanging out in the corner of the room. If nothing else, this put my blind date situation into perspective. Enduring a few more awkward encounters would be nothing compared to what Amanda was facing.

"Do you know where Marquette put the folder for the Davenport vow renewal?" Amanda asked, sifting through a pile of manila folders in her inbox.

Crossing to the assistant's desk, I did a quick search and found the folder in question. "Here you go."

As I handed it over, her eyes locked with mine and for a split second I saw fear in their blue depths. "Don't worry about the business," I said, attempting to put her at ease in any way that I could. "I'll handle everything here."

With a casual tilt of her head, she flipped the folder open. "I'm not worried." After a brief pause, she added, "About anything."

That was the first time I'd ever heard Amanda tell a lie, and I didn't blame her one bit. Sometimes you had to lie to get through the hard times. I'd been there done that and knew the trick well. Crossing back to my own desk, I sent up a little prayer to whatever higher being might be listening that she'd come through this and be back to her normal, healthy self on the other side.

We may not have been close, but she was still the woman who'd taught me everything I knew about this business and given me more freedom and autonomy in my work than I'd have found anywhere else. I owed her for that, and if manning the ship for a few months would be my contribution to helping her get better, then that's what I would do.

CHAPTER FOUR

After three morning meetings, I'd managed to squeeze in a lunchtime visit with Donna. I stopped at the Lebanese place around the corner from her building, and then showed up with gyros and a tabbouli salad in hand. Near the end of the meal, I conveyed the news about my boss.

"Who talks about cancer like that?" Donna asked as I scanned through the DeStefano engagement photos. "She didn't give any other details?"

"Nope. Just that's she's starting chemo and I'd have to take all the clients until further notice."

I wrote down the image numbers on a couple photos I thought the bride would like and continued the search, gnawing on my pita bread as I went. I needed at least five to present for their review so they could choose the one we'd frame and have at the table with the guest book. The bride wanted her guests to write little notes on the white mat that would surround their faces and planned to enclose it all under glass as a keepsake.

“Maybe she doesn’t have all the info yet,” Donna suggested. “Surely she’ll tell you more eventually.”

Would she? I wasn’t counting on it.

“You know Amanda,” I said. “She’s as forthcoming as a mob informant before the guarantee of immunity. What do you think of this one?” I pointed to a close-up shot in black and white.

She shook her head. “She won’t like her nose at that angle.”

Examining the image further, I had to agree.

As a professional wedding photographer, Donna Bradford handled all Three Rivers events except on the rare occasion when two ran consecutively. We also recommended her for engagement shots and most couples took the suggestion. A proud woman entrepreneur, she wasn’t only a friend, she was an inspiration. Starting your own business was intimidating enough. Starting it right out of college and maintaining sustained success for nearly a decade was downright badassery.

Her studio was a loft on Bedford Square that doubled as both a work and a living space. Exposed brick. Original hardwood floors. Very industrial and modern. Her apartment, a mere wall away, was the complete opposite. The same exposed brick and duct work, but a much more warm and cozy aesthetic.

"How am I supposed to limit this to five?" I asked. "She looks good in all of them." When choosing the right engagement photo, I always went with the ones that made the bride look the best. In my experience, grooms rarely cared what they looked like so long as the bride was happy.

"Of course, she does. Because I took the pictures." Donna leaned over me to slide a finger across the laptop mouse pad. Two clicks later, she said, "I pulled these ones before you got here."

Five perfect images popped up.

"Why didn't you show me these first?"

She balanced on the corner of the desk. "You don't like it when I choose them without you."

"Consider that no longer the case. If I'm going to handle my clients *and* Amanda's while heading into the full sprint of wedding season, feel free to do anything and everything that will make my life easier."

I still had no idea how I was going to manage. After reviewing my calendar, the only solution appeared to be me never sleeping again while convincing clients to take late-night meetings whenever possible. I'd also parsed out a list of tasks that could be handled with a phone call alone, but I had to make the time to make the calls. My cell would be attached to my head for the foreseeable future. Reminding myself of the reason for the extra work made me feel terrible for whining, even if only in my head.

Donna snapped the laptop shut. "That I can do. Now, about tonight. What are you wearing?"

The date. Crap. I nearly forgot.

"I haven't decided yet. Where are we meeting again?"

"Marco's on the North Shore. Whatever you do, do not wear what you have on."

I looked down at my baby-blue pencil skirt and matching blazer. "What's wrong with what I have on? This is an expensive business suit."

"*Business* being the key word," she said. "Tonight you're off the clock. Why don't you ever let your personal style show through in your work clothes?"

Much like the native accent, bohemian thrift store finds did not convey the correct tone when convincing clients to spend an extra five thousand dollars on the better booze. A decision no one ever regretted, by the way.

"Not everyone can dress like an artiste," I replied. Donna could rock absolutely any look—from skinny jeans and heels to a leather dress with thigh-high boots—and still command respect. "That said, I promise to change my clothes." *When* was the question but I'd figure that out later. "What do I need to know about this guy?"

"I've given you the basics. He lives downstairs, is a personal trainer, and is freaking gorgeous."

These facts told me nothing about him as a person. "If he's so perfect, why aren't *you* going out with him?"

Donna's dedication to her business, along with her

schedule documenting activism in the community and planning the exhibition she'd been dreaming about for at least five years left little time for dating. This was the irony of my friends insisting that I go on these dates. None of them were dating either. At least not right now. Technically speaking, I was the only one *purposely* not dating. The others were still looking. Allegedly. I had yet to see proof.

With a noncommittal shrug, she said, "He isn't my type."

From the basic description alone, he didn't sound like mine either. "Exactly how is he *my* type?"

Donna returned to her gyro. "Three reasons. He's clean. He's a morning person. And the muscles prove that he's a hard worker."

A flimsy argument but I did appreciate all three of those traits. So he sounded like a good match on paper. Josie had thought the same thing and we saw how that went. "He isn't coming off a breakup, is he?"

"Oh, I heard about the last guy. Adam hasn't had a steady girlfriend for a while so there will be no drowning his sorrows while out with you. From what I can tell by talking to Josie, the two guys are really different."

That made it sound like they were throwing random men at me just to see if one would stick. I suppose that was as good an approach to matchmaking as any.

"Well, if he stays sober, this date will already top the first," I admitted.

"That's the spirit."

There was no spirit but I played along. All I had to do was survive the next three nights and this would all be over. Then I could bury myself in work and try not to run myself ragged while keeping the business running. Not to imply that there was any silver lining to my boss' cancer diagnosis, but my schedule for the next several months would serve as an inarguable reason to refrain from dating.

How would I possibly find time for a relationship? At this point, showers and meals were already iffy, and they were much more important than finding a man.

THANKS TO HAVING to fit in the Jankowski meeting, I ended up doing exactly what Donna told me not to do. I wore my work clothes to the date. At least the business suit had some color to it. I did unbutton the jacket and the top button of my blouse in an effort to create a day to evening look. A waste of time but the best I could do.

The driver dropped me at the corner near the entrance and I scanned the crowd for my date. Donna said to look for a tall man with dark hair and lots of muscles. That described about thirty percent of the men in the immediate area. I checked the time on my phone to see that I was five minutes late. My driver had done his best but an accident on the parkway had tangled traffic for miles.

"Becca Witherspoon?" said a man behind me.

I spun around and found myself nose level with an impressive set of pecs. Tilting my head back, I found ice-blue eyes staring intently over a crooked nose. The scruff on his chin looked as if he'd applied it with makeup and a stencil. How else could he get that top line so perfectly straight?

"Yes, I'm Becca," I finally replied. "You must be Adam."

"That's me." To my surprise, he offered a fist bump, which I awkwardly returned. "Donna said you were little but wow. You're like a munchkin."

At five foot two I did *not* qualify as a munchkin, a term I was pretty sure those who did qualify found offensive. Not a great first impression.

"Should we go inside?" I asked, eager to move things along. Beyond the salad at lunch, I'd only had time for crackers between clients and my stomach had growled through my last two meetings.

"In a hurry to eat, huh? I like a girl with an appetite so long as she doesn't overdo it." Adam looked me up and down. "With your small frame you could bulk up fast. You'll need to watch that." The comment took several seconds to process, as if he'd punched me in the face, and then followed up with *have a nice day*. He left me on the sidewalk in my backward-insult haze and strolled off toward the restaurant entrance. Realizing I wasn't with him, he turned and said, "Are you coming?"

One word came to mind. *No*. But then I heard my friends telling me I never gave him a chance and resigned myself to see this through. Plastering a smile on my face, I followed him inside and was grateful he at least held the door for me. He was probably nervous and let his filter slip. A valid reason to grant him a pass. For now.

"Heya, doll," he said to the young woman at the podium. "Two for Brubeck. I put the name down a while ago."

I hated when men called women meaningless little endearments like that. Especially women in the service industry. The hostess didn't look like she appreciated the practice either, but she kept her response professional.

Checking the list, she said, "You have one more party ahead of you, but you're welcome to wait at the bar if you'd like."

Without consulting me, he said, "That works."

Again, he walked away without me and I had to hustle to catch up, squeezing through the narrow path Adam created on his way through the crowd. I didn't typically frequent places like this one. Loud. Crowded. Trendy and hip. The fact that I even used the word hip probably proved how unhip I was.

Having not been in the singles scene in my early twenties, I never learned the fine art of clubbing. And it *was* an art form. Donna and Josie had plenty of stories involving random hookups, obnoxious drunks, and various encounters in the ladies' room that always ended in some girl-power high five before dispersing back into the mass of humanity as strangers once more.

Not that Marco's was a full-fledged club, since they had a dining room and served a full menu, but the atmosphere felt the same to me.

"I'll take a Yuengling Light," Adam said to the bartender as I reached the empty stool beside him. Turning to me, he asked, "What do you want?"

"Water, please."

Thin brows nearly met over the crooked nose. "Don't be so uptight. If it's the calories you're worried about, I'll get you one of what I'm having."

"No," I assured him. "I'm not much of a drinker." And I definitely wasn't having alcohol on an empty stomach.

"Donna didn't mention that," he said, sounding as if he regretted this fix-up as much as I did.

It wasn't as if I'd suggested he couldn't drink. He could have all he wanted, but if this date turned out to be a repeat of the last, Mr. Muscles could find his own way home. He dropped onto his stool with a pout-like expression, and I felt certain I wouldn't have to find an excuse not to schedule a date number two.

"What do you do?" he asked half-heartedly as I lifted myself onto the stool. I assumed Donna would have told him at least that much.

"I'm an event planner. Weddings. Vow renewals. Retirements. Any large gathering like that."

"So you throw parties?"

I… "No, I plan events."

"Events. Parties. Same thing."

"Not really."

Our drinks arrived and Adam handed over his card. We settled into silence as the bartender left to ring him up and I again considered putting an end to this misery. He clearly wasn't enamored with me, and I felt no need to change his mind. As he scanned the area, seemingly forgetting I was even there, I tried to figure out why Donna had thought this would work. Being a morning person wasn't a personality trait. The hard worker description may have fit but he certainly wasn't putting much work into being likable.

If there'd been anything about him that reminded me of Brian, I'd have at least understood her belief that this could work, but like Peter before him, Adam paled in comparison. Not that I expected to find Brian's twin. That would be weird and a bit disturbing. But a nice, generous guy who went out of his way to make me laugh one minute while challenging me the next didn't feel like too much to ask.

As I contemplated exit strategies, my date continued to glance down the bar as if looking for my replacement. He was welcome to choose another dinner partner at any time. The scene that followed would fall into the *you can't make this stuff up category* because at the same moment that Adam eyed up a particular blond, said blonde's companion witnessed the flirty exchange and was not happy.

"What are you lookin' at?" the stranger said to Adam while rising on his stool as if he might launch himself over the bar.

This *could not* be happening.

"Not *your* ugly ass," Adam replied.

Fabulous. This was happening.

CHAPTER FIVE

"WHAT'D YOU SAY?" THE MAN DEMANDED, LEAVING HIS stool and stepping around a group of young women in order to poke my date in the chest.

"Hey now," the bartender snapped. "Take it down a notch."

Neither Neanderthal listened.

"You callin' me ugly?" the poker asked.

"Did I stutter?" replied the pokee.

As I watched this embarrassment unfold, three things ran through my mind. *Why was I going on these dates? Was the universe messing with me? And who was going to stop this standoff before someone got hurt?*

Question number three was answered almost immediately, and in a way that proved the answer to number two was a resounding *yes*.

"Take your seats, gentlemen," the arriving bouncer

said seconds before he noticed me cringing behind Adam. "Not you again?"

The bouncer was none other than Jacob the driver. I'd have pretended I didn't recognize him but lying had never been my forte.

"This jagoff was lookin' at my girl," the stranger barked before I could speak.

"Looking isn't a crime," Adam defended. "And she smiled at me first."

Maybe I could pretend I wasn't part of this.

"Call it off or you can both leave," the driver turned bouncer announced.

"This asshole can leave." Adam shoved the stranger. "I didn't do shit."

"Touch me one more time, you son of a—"

"Out." Jacob grabbed Adam by the elbow as a fellow bouncer appeared out of nowhere to handle the other guy.

"Get your hands off me." Adam jerked his arm away and bumped into a passing waitress, knocking over the two glasses on her tray which covered me in sticky alcohol and ice. My date didn't seem to notice. "You can't kick me out," he yelled, still arguing with Jacob. "I was minding my own business."

A second later his arm was twisted up behind his back and Jacob was steering him toward the exit. Not sure what else to do, I followed. The moment they stepped outside, Jacob let him go and turned in time to catch the door before it closed in my face.

"What the hell, man?" Adam said. "You think you can use some kung fu on me? I'll kick your ass, Chinaman."

Oh, hell no. I put myself between my jerk of a date and Jacob. "What did you just say?"

"You gonna break out some karate next?" he asked, ignoring my question.

"That's offensive and racist and you're lucky he hasn't shoved your head even farther up your ass than it already is," I snapped. "What is wrong with you?"

"Did you not just see him throw me out of that bar for no reason?"

"He had plenty of reasons."

"You're *my* date. You're supposed to be on *my* side."

"You sure know how to pick 'em," Jacob mumbled behind me.

I could only deal with one jerk at a time, and I wasn't finished with Adam yet. "This date is over. I suggest you try your luck at the next bar down. Maybe you'll find a woman with a caveman fetish and you'll be all set."

The brute had the nerve to look me up and down as if *I* was the piece of shit in this scenario. "Why Donna set me up with your tight ass is a mystery anyway. Have a nice life."

He strolled off down the sidewalk as I vibrated with righteous indignation. After the tree debacle, I should have reached my mortification limit where Jacob was concerned, and yet I couldn't make myself turn around.

"You didn't have to defend me like that," he said. "It's nothing I haven't heard before."

"That doesn't make it okay," I said, turning to face him. "I'm really sorry."

Glancing down the sidewalk, he said, "Did he say this was a setup?"

I nodded. "Yeah. He lives in the same building as my friend Donna."

"Does she not like you?" he asked.

I was starting to wonder that myself.

"I assume he's never shown her his true colors." She would be hearing all about his true colors and begging for my forgiveness in the near future.

Silence fell between us until he said, "At least he didn't get drunk."

Was he trying to make me feel better?

"That doesn't feel like a perk in this situation." I pulled my phone from the purse on my hip. "I guess I'll head home."

Jacob looked at his watch. "I'll take you. My shift ends in five minutes anyway."

I peeked over the phone. "I can order a car. It's fine."

"I'm already here."

"You're here as a bouncer, right? I assume that means you aren't on driving duty."

He ran a hand through his thick black hair—an insanely sexy move—before offering a broad-shouldered shrug. "The offer stands."

I'd already taken one free ride from this man. Taking two made me feel like a moocher. "Let me see how much cash I have on me." Searching through my purse, I found a ten, three ones, and three quarters. "I'm just shy of fourteen dollars. If there's an ATM close by, I can get more."

"That isn't necessary."

"I have to give you something." The words came out harsher than intended. Taking a breath, I said, "I'm sorry. I'm having a really crappy week. Will you at least accept the money that I have on me? It would make me feel better about taking the ride."

Full lips tilted up in a boyish grin, showing off a heart-stopping set of dimples.

"Not a problem," he said. While I was still breathless from the dimples, he added, "Wait here while I go clock out."

Head empty, I could do little more than nod as he went back inside. Grateful for the chance to pull myself together, I sat down on a nearby bench and closed my eyes, wondering what the odds were that the same guy could come to my rescue two dates in a row. Whatever the chances, I was relieved for the one positive the universe had tossed my way. That scene inside could have been so much worse.

"I saw you looking at him," growled a mildly familiar voice.

I opened my eyes to find the blond woman and her date exit the restaurant.

"He smiled and I smiled back," she defended, her spiked heels clicking on the concrete as she sashayed by me. "You're so damn jealous. That's the third guy you've attacked this week."

"They keep lookin' at you. I don't like it."

They were too far away for me to hear her reply, but I hoped it was something to the tune of we should see other people. Permanently.

"Here you go," Jacob said, drawing my attention from the retreating couple. He held out a small white towel. "I thought you might need this."

My hand went straight to my hair. "I forgot about the drinks." A clump of hair was stuck to my temple so the dry towel wouldn't do much, but I still appreciated the thought. "Thank you."

"You can leave it in my car, and I'll bring it back my next shift." Nodding in the direction the arguing couple had gone, he said, "My car is this way."

"Oh, right." We made our way down the sidewalk toward Heinz Field, taking a right at the end of the block. "Thanks again for doing this. My address is two hundred—"

"Cowan Street," he finished for me. "I know."

"You remember?"

"It's been forty-eight hours. Of course, I remember. How's your head?"

I tried prying a clump of hair apart. "Sticky right now."

"I meant the bump from the other night."

Touching the small bruise I'd managed to cover with my bangs that morning, I said, "Much better. I put ice on it like you suggested and that helped take the swelling down."

"Smart." He pointed to the right as we approached a large parking area. "The car is in lot two. Can I ask you a question?"

That was a question, but I'd have been a smart-ass for saying so. "Go ahead."

"What's with the blind dates?"

I was tempted to say *How much time do you have?* Instead, I gave the reason I assumed most people would have in this situation.

"Looking for love, right? Isn't that the reason anyone goes on a blind date?" This was not my reason, of course.

"I'm not asking just anyone. I'm asking you. You're attractive. A little clumsy but seemingly a good person. Why can't you find your own dates?"

How to answer that? I could, I had to assume, find a date if I really wanted to. I simply didn't want to. But saying as much would lead to more questions that I didn't want to answer.

"I'm busy," I said, hoping that would satisfy his curiosity. "Why not delegate where you can?"

He pressed a button on his key fob and the lights of a white Buick flashed, accompanied by the sound of unlocking doors. "You keep answering my questions with a question."

Stepping around to the passenger door, I said, "Maybe that's your clue to stop asking questions."

I had to give him credit. He took my borderline-rude response in stride. "Message received."

We buckled up in silence and as he drove through the North Shore streets, I watched the world go by out his passenger window for the second time that week. Being with a stranger shouldn't feel quite so comfortable, but exhaustion and hunger kept me from analyzing the situation too deeply. I'd found a good Samaritan. Twice. A strange coincidence but a coincidence nonetheless. One I greatly appreciated since all I wanted to do was go home, grab whatever I could scrounge up in my fridge, and crawl into bed.

"YOU'RE A DRIVER AND A BOUNCER THEN?" I asked once the silence stretched a little too far. We were crossing the West End Bridge so I made it at least seven minutes without talking. That's a long time for me.

"You get to ask questions?" he said, cutting me a friendly glare.

A fair response. "Yes, I do. How many other jobs do you have?"

Jacob brought the car to a stop at the light at end of the bridge. "One more."

When he didn't elaborate, I said, "And that is?"

"What do you do?" came the response.

A worthy opponent, indeed. If he wasn't telling, neither was I.

"Well played," I muttered. "You said earlier that I'm a seemingly nice person. Based on what?"

I truly had no idea how a stranger I'd spent less than an hour with could come to such a conclusion.

We rolled into motion again as he replied, "You went the extra mile to get your drunk date home the other night, and you defended me a little while ago. I guess it's possible that you might kick puppies when no one is looking, but based on our two encounters, the good person thing seemed like a safe guess."

An accurate assessment, which revealed a keen sense of observation and a willingness to see the good in people. Even clumsy strangers whose friends had terrible taste in blind dates.

"I do *not*, in fact, kick puppies when no one is looking. Or when they are looking, for that matter." Feeling as if I should return the compliment, I added, "And you seem like a good person, too. Considering you've saved me twice now. Do you find that as odd as I do?"

"That I'm a good person?"

"No, that we've run into each other twice like this." The odds had to be against us. "I mean, this is a relatively large city. What are the odds of two strangers crossing paths like this over just a few days?"

He kept his eyes on the road and eased the car left after the light. "Both run-ins have been close to the center of town so not that strange. If the first time was out in West View and the other in Bridgeville, then I'd have to wonder."

Good point. Those two areas were pretty far apart, one north and the other south of town. Chance encounters weren't completely unheard of. "You're right. This is just a weird coincidence."

"Or there's some force in the universe that keeps putting us in the same place," he countered.

The man needed to pick a lane. "For what purpose?"

"You tell me."

"It's *your* theory."

"But *you* brought it up."

Now he was just being difficult. "I don't believe the higher power idea. We've had two chance encounters, and I'm sure that after tonight, we'll never see each other again."

As he maneuvered the car onto the main strip at the top of Mount Washington, I watched the lights of downtown come into view.

"What if we do?" he asked.

I sensed that he was enjoying this exchange and so was I. More than I had during any moments with my blind dates.

"Then I'm going to assume that you're stalking me."

That got a reaction. "*I'm* stalking *you*? I'd say it's the other way around."

Nonsense. "How do you figure?"

"You ordered the car and then chose me to be your driver. Plus, how do I know you didn't leave your purse and phone in my car so that you'd have a way to find me again? As for tonight, you came into my place of work, not the other way around."

Damn it, his argument made sense. "So I'm the one perpetuating these unfortunate encounters?"

He spared me a glance, flashing the dimples that made my brain go fuzzy. "*Are* they unfortunate?"

They were on a circumstantial level. "If I hadn't been in the midst of two horrible dates, I wouldn't have needed rescuing, and you wouldn't have had to play the hero. So yes, our brief history has been unfortunate for me."

"Again, you've got that backwards. What you should say is *fortunately* for you I came along at the right time. Twice."

He hadn't been this argumentative during our first encounter and I had to admit I liked the challenge. Refusing to back down, I said, "You're taking too much credit. There would have been another driver and another bouncer."

"But there wasn't," he said, putting the car in park. "Here you go."

I looked around and realized we were sitting in front

of the door to my building. The same door where he'd dropped me two nights ago.

"I'm home."

"You are."

For some unknown reason, I didn't want to get out of the car. "Thank you for the ride," I said as I dug the cash from my purse. "We really should have stopped at an ATM on the way. There's one at the convenience store a block over. We could go now."

"Not necessary." Jacob took the bills I offered and said, "Keep the quarters."

There was no reason for me not to get out of the car and the longer I sat there, the weirder things got. For a split second I considered asking if I could see him again. This time, on purpose. But then I remembered that I knew nothing about him. He could have a girlfriend or a boyfriend or a wife or dead bodies in his basement.

It was time to go.

"Thank you again," I said, opening the door and climbing out. "If you come up in my app again, should I reject the ride and wait for the next one?"

"And rob me of another debate?" he replied.

Heart melting, I offered a genuine smile. "That would be a shame."

"Until next time then," he said with a nod.

I closed the door and stepped back for him to leave, but the car stayed put and I realized he was once again waiting until I got inside. Whoever Jacob the driver slash bouncer had waiting at home was a lucky individual. Unless they were dead in the basement, of course, but I doubted that was the case. With a last glance over my shoulder, I waved goodbye from the doorway and watched him drive off into the proverbial sunset.

Why couldn't my friends find me someone like him? They had two more tries but based on the choices so far, I was not holding my breath. By the time I reached the second-floor landing, I'd decided that a conversation needed to happen beforehand if I was going to try this date thing for a third time. And that conversation needed to happen tonight.

CHAPTER SIX

By the time I reached my apartment, I decided to put off the call long enough to eat something. Life had been so crazy lately, I wasn't even sure what I had in the house. Stepping inside, I heard a noise coming from my kitchen and froze. Milo didn't make that kind of noise.

Like the first to die in every horror movie ever, I said, "Hello?"

"Hello?" came the response.

Rolling my eyes, I closed the door and dropped my keys in the glass dish on the entry table. "Why are you in my apartment?" I asked, rounding the corner to find Josie holding a bowl of cereal and wearing a guilty look on her face.

"I was out of milk," she replied. "Why are you home so early?"

"Because my date got us kicked out of the restaurant before we were even seated." Dropping my purse onto the table, I took the bowl from her hands. "I've had nothing but a salad today and I'm starving. Make yourself a new bowl."

Josie didn't argue nor did she reach for the cereal.

"Why didn't you eat more than that?" she asked, following me to the couch. That was not the part of the story I'd expected her to question first.

"Because I had to pick up some of Amanda's meetings and there wasn't time."

I hadn't seen Josie since Amanda dropped her cancer announcement on me. Would she care that I told my friends? She hadn't asked me to keep the news to myself, and she didn't exactly socialize with my friends so there didn't seem to be much harm in sharing.

"When are you going to tell that demanding woman to hire someone else?" Josie snapped. "Becca, you can't keep letting her run you to death like this. She should have hired another planner years ago."

A drop of milk landed on my chin and I used my sleeve to dab it away. She was right, of course, and I'd mentioned increasing the staff to Amanda before. She'd insisted that we could handle things on our own. Even hiring Marquette had taken nearly a year of begging, and he'd only been with us for eighteen months.

"She has cancer," I said, unfairly dropping the bomb on Josie just as Amanda had dropped it on me.

I swayed as she plopped onto the couch beside me. "She what?"

"Has cancer," I enunciated. "All I know is that she's starting an aggressive treatment and needs me to handle her clients for the next couple months. She didn't even tell me what kind so I have no other information."

"That's awful and I hope she's okay, but this is your busiest time of year. You can't handle all of that on your own."

Stating the obvious, I said, "I don't have a choice."

"Tell her you can't."

I couldn't do that anymore than I could tell my friends to stop pushing me into these dates. I was literally incapable of saying no to anyone. If Adam hadn't been such a jerk to Jacob, I'd probably still be suffering through his nauseating company.

"I can't tell a woman who is potentially dying that she'll have to find someone else to keep her business running while she goes through chemo." It wasn't as if I hadn't thought this through. "I've looked at my schedule and I can make it work so long as the clients are flexible with meetings. Every venue has a stellar rep that I've worked with before, and I trust them to handle most of the detail work. Marquette has been asking for more responsibility so this is the perfect time to let him have it."

"I thought Amanda told him no."

"She did." A mere wrinkle in my plan. "But if she's

going to be too busy to handle her clients, I'm assuming she won't be around to know exactly what's happening in the office either. By the time she comes back, we'll have documented proof that Marquette is fully capable of taking on his own clients."

I looked down and realized my cereal had gotten soggy. I hated soggy cereal.

"Here," Josie said, taking the bowl before I could complain. "You need real food anyway. Tell me about this date while I make you some eggs and toast."

Eggs and toast sounded much better than cold cereal.

"Did you guys discuss the men you picked for these dates?" I asked as Josie shuffled into the kitchen and Milo strolled out of the bedroom to finally say hello. "Because if these were picked by committee, I might have to shop around for new friends."

"Not exactly," she replied, gathering the items she needed onto the counter. As the frying pan landed on the stove, she added, "We talked a little."

"Meaning you talked about finding guys who wouldn't remind me of Brian," I stated, knowing that's what she was dancing around.

We'd all been dancing around this subject for two years, and I seemed to be the only person willing to even say his name. My friends pretended Brian never existed. At least they did when I was in the room. I doubted that was the case when I wasn't.

Josie froze with the carton of eggs halfway to the

counter. She looked as if she'd been caught in the middle of a burglary and told not to move.

"Why don't you guys ever say his name?" I asked. Why I picked this moment to bridge the subject I didn't know. Maybe I was just too tired to maintain the dance.

Setting the eggs on the counter, Josie stared at my backsplash for several seconds before turning around. "When you see that someone has a painful wound, you don't stick your finger in it," she said. "Especially when you care about the person deeply and you wish you could have protected them better."

I never wanted anyone to feel guilty for my misfortunes. Well, one person, but he'd given himself the ultimate punishment before I could do it for him.

"None of you could have protected me from what happened."

"No," she agreed, "but we can protect you now."

"There's nothing to protect me *from*," I said, kicking off my shoes and slipping out of my jacket. In a full stretch, I added, "Except these dates you guys keep picking. And low-hanging sycamore branches, apparently."

Taking the cue that I was done talking about the past, Josie went back to making eggs while Milo leaped onto my lap and starting kneading himself a place on my stomach.

"What happened tonight?" Josie asked. "How do you get kicked out of a restaurant?"

"My date got into an altercation with another patron,"

I replied. “Donna’s neighbor was not impressed by me *at all*, and before we were even seated, he started making eyes at a woman in the bar. Her boyfriend took umbrage to this and the two men began insulting and poking each other.”

“Poking?” she repeated.

“Yes. Poking. Security stepped in and the next thing I knew, we were outside, where Adam was a complete douche to the bouncer who had to physically remove him.”

I considered adding more details about the bouncer, but something stopped me. I didn’t want to share Jacob with her. I doubted I could talk about him without sounding interested and that was like throwing a bone to a starving dog. My friends would jump on the mystery man narrative and maybe even try to find him.

Jacob would stay my little secret. My knight in a white Buick with the perfect dimples, heart-melting brown eyes, and a knack for healthy debate. The first two were nice bonuses, but the third was the real attraction. Funny that my closest friends couldn’t pair me up with anyone even half as perfect for me, yet the first guy I would willingly spend any time with I’d found totally by accident.

And would likely never see again.

Life liked to toss me little ironies like that. To give and then to take away. Whatever I did in a past life to deserve this particular punishment must have been really bad. Maybe my former self did kick puppies when no one was looking. Or maybe I was a femme fatale who lured men away from their wives. Or I was just a lowly peasant who had it much worse off than I did now.

"Wait a second. Did you say he tried to pick up another woman while you were sitting there?"

"Technically, he only smiled at her. I have no idea what would have happened if she'd been alone." Setting Milo on the couch, I slid to my feet and crossed to the kitchen, stepping around Josie to reach the fridge. "I honestly don't know what Donna was thinking. At least Peter was a nice guy." Filling a glass from my filtered water pitcher, I added, "Have you seen him since Tuesday?"

"Once," she replied while pouring the egg mixture into the hot pan. "We ran into each other at the copier and he practically ran in the other direction. Oh, and I'm having lunch with Evelyn next week. Turns out she loves Asian dramas as much as we do. We got to talking and I thought about what you said. The next thing I knew I was suggesting we have lunch."

"Good for you."

"Becca, what's in your hair?" Josie leaned closer and touched a curl near my ear. "Why is it sticky?"

I'd forgotten about that. "Oh, yeah. Adam bumped a waitress on our way out and I wore the drinks on her tray. I'm going to take a shower, and then we're having a little group chat while I eat."

Eyes wide, she said, "A group chat? About what?"

Years ago we'd established the group chat rule. When one of us was at a breaking point, the rest would stop whatever they were doing to gather by whatever means necessary to deal with the problem. A couple of bad blind dates weren't necessarily enough to trigger the chat, but with two more dates looming, I was elevating the situation to emergency status.

"The next two dates," I replied, putting the pitcher back in the fridge. "I trusted you guys to pick these men and so far, you're oh for two. Unless I hear something real damn convincing, I'm pulling the plug on the rest."

"But you agreed to this," she argued. "How are you going to find the right one if you aren't willing to endure some not great ones along the way?"

I lifted my bangs and pointed at my head. "Not great?" I repeated. "This is more than not great, Josie. This is a massive contusion currently being covered by vodka-soaked hair."

"Fine," she conceded. "But I'm sure Megan and Lindsey's picks are better. What if one of them is *the* guy and you miss your chance to meet him?"

The odds of that were so slim I didn't justify the question with a response. "Just round up the troops. I won't be long."

As I collected the clothes I needed to take into the bathroom, exhaustion nearly took me down, but I was determined to push through to get this date thing straightened out. Unless Megan and Lindsey were absolutely certain that the men they'd picked were reasonably sane, nonviolent, and not on the rebound, my blind dating days were over.

HAIR still wet from my shower, I finished off my eggs as the girls pled their cases on why the rest of the dates weren't a waste of my time. Josie and I were on my laptop while Megan, Donna, and Lindsey were each on their phones. Thanks to modern technology, we no longer had to gather at someone's house—or dorm room—like in the earlier days.

"You can't give up after two blind dates," Megan argued. Her dark hair was held back by a blue headband sporting a unicorn horn, and gray goop covered her face. The emergency chat had interrupted her pampering time. "There are still two more to go, and I'm sure these will be better."

If I believed that, we wouldn't be having this conversation.

"I agree," Lindsey said, waving a cheese puff as she spoke. Lindsey Pavolski was my oldest and closest friend, and responsible for choosing date number four. That poor guy would be the literal embodiment of a last-ditch effort. That was *if* the date happened at all, which was unlikely unless they changed my mind. "You can't call off our picks just because Josie and Donna have awful taste."

"Hey!" Josie and Donna said in unison.

"Hey, what?" Lindsey snapped back. "Am I wrong?" Neither woman had a defense so Lindsey continued. "That's what I thought. Becca, I get that the first two weren't for you, and that sucks, but you agreed to four dates. I don't know about Megan's pick, but I promise that my guy is perfect for you."

"My guys is pretty great, too," Megan claimed.

I'd heard them out, but now it was time for the cross-examination.

"Megan, I'll start with you. *How* do you know him and *what* is so great about him?"

She blinked as if I'd suggested she recite the Russian alphabet. "Well..." she hedged. "He's a writer who comes to the book group I run at the library. He's very smart. And he's sweet. Just the other day he brought cupcakes to our book club meeting, and despite the fact that we couldn't eat them because food isn't allowed in the library, it was still a nice thought."

Generous with desserts was a plus, but not enough to make him worth the date.

"What else?"

"What else?" she repeated, lips pursed. "He always has great insight into the books we read. Last month we read *Pride and Prejudice* and he pointed out how Darcy forgiving Elizabeth for her crush on Wickham proved how much he cared about her. No one else in the group even thought of that."

This was not a point in his favor. Everyone knew there was no forgiveness necessary since Darcy understood firsthand how conniving and manipulative Wickham could be. Plus, once Elizabeth knew the other man's true nature, her feelings completely changed. But fine. The potential date was entitled to his own erroneous opinion.

"Has he recently broken up with anyone?" I queried, not wanting a repeat of date number one. Looking to avoid another version of date number two as well, I added, "And does he have more muscles than manners?"

"Why would I pick a guy with muscles?" she asked. "You don't even like that." Donna rolled her eyes but embraced her right to remain silent. "There are no recent girlfriends that I know of," Megan continued. "He's been coming to the book club for about six months and has never mentioned anyone. Oh, and he's a total gentleman. Holds the door. Always helps stack the chairs after meetings. That sort of thing."

He did sound better than the previous options. Not good enough to make me consider taking the date seriously, but an evening talking about books would be a vast improvement on my week so far.

"You're certain you can't think of any reason why this date could go south? Anything at all?"

She shook her head. "Nothing, I promise."

Scrunching up her nose, Megan leaned closer to her camera. "I need to go wash off this mask before it gets any drier. I'll be right back." She promptly disappeared, leaving us staring at the Squirtle plushy on her headboard. A love of everything Pokémon was Megan's one unexpected quirk.

"Now it's your turn, Lindsey." I gathered the last of my eggs onto my fork. "Same questions. Go."

Closing the cheese puff bag, she licked her orange fingertips before answering. "I know him from school." Lindsey taught English at our former high school. "He's in the social studies department and teaches mostly AP classes. I can't claim to know his entire dating history, but I do know that he hasn't been in a relationship for as long as I've known him and that's two years." Carrying her phone, she took us with her into her kitchen. "He has impeccable manners, and the kids don't just love him, they respect him. That's a feat few of us achieve."

We got a shot of her ear as she shoved the puffs bag into her pantry. "He has this easy air about him. Like, you just feel… comfortable with him. It's hard to explain but I'm telling you, your personalities are a perfect fit."

He actually sounded kind of nice. Dang it, this conversation was supposed to end with me calling off these dates. I hadn't expected my friends to make such solid arguments.

When I didn't say anything, Josie bumped my shoulder. "I think you girls convinced her."

Megan returned at that moment and said, "What? What did I miss?"

"She's going on the dates," Donna said, leaning back on her couch and holding the phone above her head. "Am I ever going to live down picking this neighbor? I had no idea he was such a jerk."

"No," the four of us said.

She huffed. "Fair enough. Maybe I'll get lucky and he'll move before I see him in the hall again."

"What are you going to say when you do see him?" Josie asked.

"I have no idea, but it won't be nice."

Sitting up again, Donna rose to her feet, showing only her forehead on the screen. "I have more pictures to edit so I'm getting off here. Becca, I really am sorry."

I couldn't blame her if Adam never showed his douchey side while chatting at the mailboxes. "It's okay, Donna." Trying to lighten the mood, I added, "But I probably won't ever agree to let you set me up again."

"No worries there. I am *out* of the matchmaking business." Showing her face once more, she said, "Sweet dreams, ladies."

Everyone returned the sentiment and Donna disappeared.

CHAPTER SEVEN

"WE SHOULDN'T HAVE BEEN SO MEAN," MEGAN mumbled, ever the sensitive heart.

"The dude tried to hit on another woman, and then picked a fight with a bouncer," Lindsey reiterated, as if Megan had just tuned in. "Becca let her off way easier than I would have."

Lindsey could best be described as the hard-ass of the group. She held others to a high standard, but was harder on herself than anyone else. She did not tolerate fools, hated small talk, and could hold a grudge for decades. Mention of the bouncer made me think of Jacob and I realized if I hadn't agreed to these dates, I might never have met him. Not that meeting him was anything monumental, but our brief encounters were the only positives to come out of these things.

"Josie is right," I cut in. "I'll go on the next date, but

if anything crazy happens, I get an out on date number four."

"Absolutely not." Lindsey dropped her phone on something, giving us a shot of the fluorescent light on her kitchen ceiling. "I've wanted to set you up with this guy for a year, but I knew you weren't ready. Now you are and I'm not letting you out of this." We heard her fridge open and close before she continued. "If I'm wrong, I'll clean your apartment for the next six months."

Seconds passed in silence before Megan said, "Wow. She must really be sure about this."

We all knew Lindsey hated to clean. Even on her meager teaching salary, she found a way to pay for a cleaning service twice a month. She did the bare minimum in between—ran the dishwasher and did laundry—but if it weren't for the service, none of us would willingly visit her apartment. We'd even held a group chat two years ago as a cleaning intervention.

"Are you serious?" I asked. Because I fully planned to hold her to that promise.

"Absolutely," she said, picking the phone back up and taking us with her across her living room. "I have thirty papers to grade before morning so I need to go. Is this settled?"

The other two held silent, waiting for me to answer. "I'll go on the dates," I conceded.

"Good." Holding the phone high enough for us to see her face, she said, "Love you, all. Good night."

As Lindsey left the chat, Josie put her arm around my shoulders and said, "So, Megan, what are you going to promise if your date screws up?"

"Hey," she whined. "Your guy nearly gave her a concussion. What are you doing to make up for *that*?"

"No need to keep this going." Josie waved at the screen. "Talk to you later, Meg." She closed the window before our friend had the chance to push for an answer. I turned her way, not ready to let her off the hook. "What?" Josie said, attempting to look innocent. "You said the tree thing wasn't his fault."

"If he hadn't gotten so drunk that I had to get him home, I never would have run into the tree in the first place."

"I said I was sorry. At least you got an actual meal with my guy. That's better than Donna did, right?"

Good point. Of the two, Peter had at least been a decent guy. If he hadn't been pining over Evelyn, we might even have ended the date as friends.

"Yes, that's better than the Adam fiasco." I closed the laptop and got to my feet. "I need to go in early in the morning, and there are still a few files to review before bed. Think good thoughts about tomorrow, because regardless of what I told Lindsey, if this date is as bad as the first two, I really am putting my foot down about Saturday."

I'd never put my foot down about anything, but even I

had a limit, and these dates were pushing me right up to that line.

"It doesn't sound like Lindsey will take no for an answer," Josie said.

"She's going to have to. This is still my life, regardless of what everyone else seems to think."

Following me to the kitchen, where I put my plate in the sink, she said, "We just want you to be happy again."

Ironic, since I was willingly making myself miserable just to make *them* happy. "I don't need a man to be happy, Josie. I like my life the way it is. I have a job I love, a great family, and four dear friends who I really wish would trust me when I say that I'm fine."

Tucking a wet lock behind my ear, Josie shook her head. "You aren't fine, Becks." When I opened my mouth to argue, she silenced me with a finger pressed against my lips. "You haven't been fine for two years. No one knows you like we do, remember? We want to see that light in your eyes again. I agree that you don't need a man to be happy, but you do need to move on, and we just want to show you that love can happen again. Don't give up yet, okay?"

I had no idea what light she was talking about, but there *was* a side of me that believed love was part of my past not my future. Imagining myself with someone new felt… wrong.

"We push because we love you," she added.

I sighed. "I love you guys, too, but I really am fine."

Josie tapped my cheek. "Oh, girlfriend, you are so far from fine. And when you realize that fact for yourself, I promise not to say I told you so."

Rolling my eyes, I shoved her toward the exit. "When these dates are over, I promise to remind you guys *at every opportunity* what you put me through. Now be gone. I have work to do."

She blew me a kiss from the hallway. "You're going to thank us if Lindsey's pick is as good as she makes him sound."

"Yeah, yeah, yeah."

I closed the door and turned the deadbolt, then grabbed my bag of files and shuffled into my bedroom. Crawling onto my bed, I scattered a stack of folders onto my comforter and arranged them in the order the meetings took place the next day. This required accommodating Milo in the center of the mattress. Flipping the first one open, I tried to concentrate on reviewing the status report inside, but Lindsey's words kept playing in my head.

...you just feel... comfortable with him.

I'd already met someone recently who fit that description. Too bad he wasn't the date. Jacob's dimples danced through my mind and I shook the image away. I didn't even know the man, and the chances of ever seeing him again were slim to none. These files weren't going to review themselves so I forced myself to focus.

In two days this would be over. Just two more days.

WE DIDN'T NORMALLY OPEN the office until eight, but I went in at seven to knock out some emails before my day started. Before Amanda's news, I'd had three meetings scheduled but now I had five. Not a high number, but due to the distance between them, I'd have no time to return to the office.

I also came in early so I could update Marquette. I wasn't happy to be the bearer of bad news and I had no idea how he would take it. He wouldn't be happy, of course, but this situation created a lot of uncertainty surrounding the business. What if her clients didn't want to work with someone else? What if the treatment didn't work and she had to be away longer? Or worse yet, never came back? I couldn't imagine Three Rivers Events without Amanda at the helm. Then again, if the worst *did* happen, the business would likely be dissolved or sold. Then where would Marquette and I be?

I felt selfish even thinking such a thing, but if she'd shared a few more details, my mind wouldn't be racing through every possible scenario. What-ifs were still spinning through my head when an odd noise caught my attention. It sounded like a tire with a slow leak.

"Psssst." My fingers hovered above the keyboard as the sound was followed by, "Is she here?"

"No, Marquette, Amanda isn't here, but we need to talk."

"We sure as hell do." He crossed to his desk and dropped his Gucci bag in a bottom drawer. "Why didn't you tell me?"

How could he have possibly heard already?

"Tell you what?" I hedged, not wanting to make any assumptions. I knew how it felt to have this news dropped with the brevity of a weather forecast.

Concern creased his features. "Oh, my God. You don't know?"

"Do you mean why Amanda isn't here?"

"I mean that the woman has cancer," he blurted.

Was there some billboard that I didn't know about? "How do *you* know?"

"She emailed me," he said, eyes wide and brows arched to his hairline. "Who the hell tells you they have cancer via email?"

Oh, Amanda, how could you? "She told you in an email?"

"Yes!" he exclaimed. "I nearly fell over on the bus and dropped my phone."

On one hand, this spared me from being the bearer of bad news. On the other, I shared Marquette's outrage.

"What else did she say?"

Marquette crossed his arms and dropped a hip onto the corner of his desk. "Absolutely nothing. Just that she has cancer and that you'd be in charge for the next couple of months."

In charge? That was new. I'd expected her to still be

around, at least part of the time. Amanda had never left me in charge of anything, and I wasn't sure I wanted the responsibility. She should have at least discussed it with me. On a positive note, this did give me the power to increase Marquette's duties.

"I don't know anything else either."

"She didn't give you the details?" he asked, his voice rising another octave.

Staring at the empty desk across the room, I shook my head. "Nothing. Just that it's cancer and she'll be off for treatment."

Marquette threw his hands in the air. "I don't expect her to tell me anything, but she owes you more than that. What the hell?"

Did she, though? This lack of sharing was consistent with our established relationship. Sometime during the last eight years, we'd created an unwritten rule to keep things business only. Until now, the lack of personal connection hadn't bothered me, but this wasn't the same as not chatting about holidays with the family or some new drama we were enjoying.

This was cancer and possibly life or death. A damn good reason to break the rule. Apparently, Amanda didn't see it that way.

"If she doesn't want to tell us, then that's her prerogative. What we have to figure out now is how to keep this place running while she's gone."

"I can work more hours to keep things organized here," he offered.

Time to test the waters. "Actually, I was thinking more like having you work closer with clients."

The perfectly sculpted brows arched again. "Are you serious? Will Amanda approve that?"

"She said I'm in charge, right? There's no way I can handle every single client and event by myself. Even when Amanda is here, there aren't enough hours in the day. How could she not approve?"

To be fair, I had no idea why she'd objected up to now. Marquette was a bit of a character, but he was professional, knew every detail of every event we planned, and had the perfect personality to engage with clients. Several already loved him just from dealing with him over the phone.

Before Marquette could comment on my plan, Amanda walked through the door and charged to her desk as if this was any other day.

"Morning," she said, sparing neither of us a glance.

Marquette caught my eye and mouthed *What the hell?* I didn't have an answer.

"Good morning," I responded. Unsure of what else to say, I asked, "How are you?"

She looked at me as if I'd said something odd. "I'm fine. Why?"

"Well… I…" Saying because you have cancer didn't seem polite. "Just asking," I finally finished.

"How did the Jankowski meeting go yesterday?"

"Good," I replied. "They're happy with the venue and the hall has no problem with us bringing in a large screen to show the old home movies."

The elderly couple planned to celebrate seventy years of wedded bliss surrounded by one hundred and fifty of their closest friends and family. The visual walks down memory lane had been their only nonnegotiable request.

"Excellent. I've gathered and updated all of the folders for events I have coming in the next three months." She dropped a small file box onto my desk. "They're in order by event date. Purple means wedding. Blue means corporate. Green means everything else. All of the information is here so there will be no need to go through my desk." She glanced from me to Marquette and back. "Understand?"

"Yes," we said in stereo.

"Good."

As she crossed back to her desk, Marquette nodded aggressively in her direction. I knew what he wanted but maybe this was one of those times when asking for forgiveness instead of permission was the smarter way to go. Unfortunately, our ambitious assistant didn't get the hint.

"Before you came in, Becca was saying how this is a good time for me to work closer with the clients. Maybe even take over a few projects to help out."

"No," Amanda snapped.

Why couldn't he have kept his mouth shut?

I cleared my throat. "What I said was that getting through the next couple of months might be easier if Marquette takes on a little more responsibility. This is our busiest time and—"

"Marquette will continue as usual," Amanda said, cutting me off. "The remaining events this month have all been finalized. The ones in June only need the last-minute confirmations done. Our calendar is lighter in July so that shouldn't be an issue."

How was she forgetting the bulk of the work? "I'm still having to meet with clients for events through the rest of the year, plus locking in venues for next year. Then there's the requests we get weekly for potential new business."

Amanda tucked her chair under her desk without ever sitting down. "There won't be any new business. I'm closing to new clients until further notice."

My entire body went numb. No new clients? That would bring the business to a stand still.

"You're what?" I said.

Ignoring the question, she pulled her purse onto her shoulder and tossed the beige trench coat over her arm. "I'll stop by a couple of days next week; otherwise, if you need to contact me, use email."

She couldn't just leave after such an announcement. I dashed from my chair and followed her to the door. "Are you planning to close this business?"

Spinning on her heels, which forced me to step back in order to tilt my head far enough to make eye contact, she stared at me for a full five seconds before answering. "My goal is to keep this business going for as long as possible, and I'm making decisions to that end. I trust *you* to make sure I still have a business when this is over. Can you or can you not do that?"

The smack from the sycamore had been less painful.

"Of course," I said, my voice small as I tried to fold in on myself.

Without another word, she breezed through the door and silence loomed around me. Loud and heavy and suffocating. Where did I get off demanding answers at a time like this? And asking such a selfish question? Ending up unemployed wouldn't be nearly as bad as what could happen to her.

"You okay?" Marquette asked, startling me out of my downward spiral.

"I'm fine," I said, returning to my seat when the alarm on my phone went off. "I have to order the car for my first meeting. I probably won't make it back in today."

Pausing with my hands braced on the back of my chair, I filled my lungs and focused on a sticky note stuck to the bottom of my monitor. My therapist had suggested I put it there two years ago and I still relied on the words written across it.

You can breathe your way through anything.

"I'll take care of things here," Marquette assured me, his voice that of a teacher soothing a frightened child.

Looking up, I recalled myself saying those same words two days before and uttered the response I wished Amanda had said to me.

"Thank you."

CHAPTER EIGHT

I REALLY DID LOVE MY JOB, BUT ONE OF THE DOWNSIDES to enduring one meeting after the next was the need to constantly smile. My cheeks ached from the effort so the time in between, when I didn't have to be on, was often my favorite part of the day. I managed to carve out thirty minutes around mid-afternoon to grab a late lunch, and after finding a table at the back of the restaurant patio, I massaged my face with one hand while scrolling through the notifications on my phone with the other.

The phone had been dinging for hours but other than making sure there were no 9-1-1 messages from Marquette, I hadn't taken the time to read them. The first was a text from Megan letting me know my date was looking forward to meeting me. I wished I could say the same. She included a brief description, which I appreciated, and a few more pertinent details we hadn't discussed the night before.

In addition to Chad being a writer from the book club at her library, he was a Georgetown grad originally from our area and currently working customer service. More power to him. I tried that one summer during college and quickly learned I was not cut out for that level of abuse. She estimated him to be around five foot seven, so at least I wouldn't have to crimp my neck all night to maintain eye contact. Short brown hair, hazel eyes, and a kind smile.

The last message read, "*Like I said,* n*othing like the last two*," and included a picture of this perfectly nice-sounding man.

The description fit and some of the anxiety about the night eased since harmless was the first word that came to mind. Though I had to wonder why we were meeting at a sports bar. The Pens were playing the Capitals—our conference rivals—in a playoff game tonight in DC which meant the bar would be packed with rowdy fans. I appreciated getting to watch the game, but Chad didn't look like the hockey type.

Not that there necessarily was such a thing as a hockey type. The times I'd attended in person I'd been surrounded by fans ranging from five to seventy-five, all passionate about the game and the players they supported. No reason Chad couldn't be one of them.

The next message was from Mom. Aunt Jeanne, my

dad's youngest sister, was coming to stay for a while and would be moving into my old bedroom. Mom had apparently found a box of my things in the closet and was going to have Joey drop it off at my place. I had no clue what would be inside and was tempted to tell her to toss it, but curiosity won out.

What's in the box? I text back.

Seconds passed before she replied. *I don't know. I didn't open it.*

I would only a few blocks away so it made sense to swing over after the date. *I'll be at Rigby's tonight. I'll stop by and go through it.*

See you then, she wrote back.

This visit would offer the added bonus of getting more details about Aunt Jeanne. Two weeks ago I got the message that she was leaving her husband after forty-two years. Either she'd decided not to stay in the house they'd shared for nearly all of those four decades, or the stay with Mom and Dad was temporary while Uncle Reginald moved out. Would he still be my uncle after they divorced? I had no idea how that worked.

Scrolling, next up was a one-line message from Lindsey.

Call me when you get this.

Hopefully, this was good news about the final date. As in, the guy changed his mind and I was off the hook. School let out twenty minutes ago so she should have been free to talk.

Answering on the second ring, she said, “Hey, lady.”

“Hey, yourself. I got your message. What’s up?”

“I just wanted to check in,” she said. “Stay in your lane, dipshit.”

I assumed the second part was not directed at me. Mild-mannered teacher by day, Lindsey turned into a foul-mouthed road-rager behind the wheel. If her students ever heard the language that crossed her lips while driving, they’d never see her in the same light again.

“Check in about what?” *Tell me he canceled. Tell me he canceled.*

“About the date.” Yes. I was off the hook. “He’s a bit reluctant.”

“I don’t blame him.” The man was obviously smarter than I was and getting out while the getting was good. “It’s fine. You gave it your best shot.”

“I didn’t say the date was off,” she snapped, bursting my balloon. “He’s just taking a little more convincing than I expected.”

Because who didn’t want to go on a date with a guy who took extra convincing to go out with you? “Just tell him to forget it, Linds. If he doesn’t want to go, he shouldn’t have to.”

I heard the *tatink, tatink* of her blinker seconds before she snapped, “Green means go, asshole. It’s the pedal under your right foot.”

“Have you tried the breathing exercises we talked about?” I asked.

"Don't be a smart-ass. These people can't freaking drive."

"You've been saying that since we were sixteen." Incidentally, riding around with teenage Lindsey had played a large part in my decision *not* to get a license. "I'm serious about the date. I don't want to spend the evening with a guy who would rather be anywhere else."

"Don't worry. I've already made the reservation on the Clipper for the six o'clock dinner cruise."

"A dinner cruise?" She hadn't mentioned this before. "If this doesn't go well, I won't be able to get away from him. What the heck, Linds?"

"You won't want to get away from him. I told you last night that he's perfect for you. Look," she said, "I've known you since we were twelve. If I can't pick out the right guy for you, then no one can."

My brain flashed back fifteen years to the moment when she'd pointed out a boy from her homeroom class and made the same claim—that he was perfect for me. That boy had been Brian, and she had been right. But just as lightning never struck twice, finding the perfect guy a second time around was not going to happen.

"Just do me a favor and don't force him, okay?"

Before she could answer, the alarm went off on my phone.

"What's that?" she asked.

"I need to order a car to get to my next meeting."

"The offer to teach you to drive is always open."

Before I could respond she growled, "Keep riding my ass, jagoff, and you'll be buying me a new car."

How did she miss the irony of uttering those two statements back-to-back?

"If common sense prevails and this date backs out," I said, "let me know. My schedule is crazy right now so having a night to catch up would be helpful."

"He'll be there, and you're going to thank me for making you do this."

Highly doubtful. "I need to go. Try not to rage your way into an accident, and keep me posted about tomorrow."

"Will do, sweetie. Good luck with your meetings and have a nice time tonight, but not too nice. Make sure my guy still has a chance."

No one had a chance and the sooner my friends admitted that, the more peaceful my life would be. With luck, Lindsey's pick would make the right choice and spare us both the hassle.

DATE NUMBER three put me back in my old stomping grounds of Carnegie. I got smart this time and brought a pair of jeans to work since we were meeting at Rigby's Irish Pub, a casual place I knew well, and one where I'd stand out like a Browns fan at a Steelers game if I walked in wearing a business suit.

The popular eatery had a long bar area at the entrance with a vintage metal tile ceiling and the kind of woodwork you didn't find in anything not built in the last century. What felt like forever ago, Dad used to bring me here to watch Pirate games in the summers when I was out of school. Back then, nobody flinched at a nine-year-old eating peanuts while her dad and his buddies downed Iron City beers and aged Irish whiskey.

The spacious and open covered patio connected to the right side of the Kelly-green building—dubbed Rigby's Garden—was a newer addition and I could see the giant screen TVs as I waited for Chad near a tree not far from the garden entrance. The pregame was still rolling but the crowd was already rowdy enough for me to hear countless conversations ranging from who would score the first goal to how badly the Pens were going to wipe the ice with the Capitals.

At the table just over the short brick wall, three older men sat beneath a black and gold patio umbrella swapping stories about previous Stanley Cup runs. They talked about the 1992 finals when the Pens routed the Blackhawks in four the way I'd heard women talk about their wedding days. The men could probably rattle off stats from that series much quicker than they could name the bridesmaids in attendance at their own nuptials.

"I'm telling you, ain't nobody ever going to top Mario," one declared.

"You don't think Sid is just as good?" a tablemate

asked with an incredulous look on his scruff-covered face.

"He's good," the first man replied, hands in the air palms forward. "I ain't saying nuttin' against him. But Mario is still my man."

The last of the threesome lifted a tall mug of beer. "Yinz can keep your fancy-ass favorites. My boy Trottier put 'em all to shame."

Bryan Trottier was Dad's favorite player of all time so I had to agree.

Leaning my back against the tree, I checked the time on my phone. Still five minutes before the meet-up time of seven so I did a quick scroll of email and found a message from Amanda.

"*I need you to cover the Henderson graduation party tomorrow. The folder is on your desk.*"

Damn it. There went my event free weekend. Sending a quick text, I asked what time the event was scheduled to run, and Amanda responded immediately with the brief reply of noon to three. That would leave plenty of time before the last date, or, if the date didn't happen, I might actually get an entire evening to sit in one place. There would be a computer on my lap, but a night on my couch with Milo purring in my ear sounded heavenly.

"Becca Witherspoon?"

I looked up from the phone to find Chad standing in front of me. As our eyes met, a wide smile split his face, and I couldn't remember the last time anyone looked so happy to see me.

"Yes, I'm Becca. Are you Chad?"

"I am." He extended a hand instead of moving in for a hug. A bonus point already. "Megan said you were cute, but your picture doesn't do you justice."

Heat rising in my cheeks, I struggled to accept the compliment. Something I'd never been good at. "Thank you. You're a handsome guy yourself."

He was slimmer than Brian with a face that made him look younger than he probably was. Nice eyes that crinkled at the corners just the right amount. And thin, but not overly so, with a cyclist's physique.

"I'm pretty ordinary, but thanks." Chad motioned toward the entrance. "Should we go in? I don't want to miss the puck drop."

"Of course. So you're a hockey fan?" I said as we walked side by side.

"Big-time. I spent a year with my grandparents in Canada when I was a kid and fell in love with the sport. I even got to play some while I was there." He paused his story to ask the hostess for a table for two. When she told us to follow her, he gestured for me to go first, and then followed behind. So far, Chad had showed more manners than the previous two dates combined. "Are you a fan?" he asked as we reached the table.

"I grew up in a sports loving family so I didn't really

have a choice." The waitress left us with two menus, and I asked, "Have you been here before?"

"Quite often, actually. I live around the corner."

"Really? I grew up a few blocks from here."

"Megan said you were from Carnegie but didn't mention which part."

Before I could reply, a group two tables away began whistling and yelling in support of the Pens. All but one in the group was wearing a team jersey. That one seemed familiar, but I could only see the back of his head. Assuming he was probably an old classmate, I returned my attention to Chad, whose was watching me with a sour expression.

"Do you know them?" he asked, all traces of the earlier smile gone.

"I might," I said. "Every now and then I see someone I went to school with when I'm over here."

He leaned back and crossed his arms. "Do you want to go sit with them?"

Strange question. "No, of course not."

"Good evening, folks," said the waiter who stepped up to the table. "Can I start you off with some drinks?"

Chad remained silent so I said, "I'd like a Sprite, please."

"I'll have a Guinness," my date snapped. "And the Rueben."

"Guinness and a Rueben," the waiter repeated. "Do you know what you'd like to eat, ma'am?"

I went with my regular order. "I'll have the grilled cheese, thanks."

"Yes, ma'am. I'll put this in and be right back with those drinks."

Silence fell over the table as the waiter walked off, and I had to wonder what happened to my friendly date. The first few minutes had gone so well. I may not have been looking for a love connection, but was one pleasant meal too much to ask?

"Megan says you're a writer," I said, looking for a topic that might get him talking again.

"Yes," he said, turning his chair to face the big screen. "The game is starting."

So we were supposed to sit here and watch the game in silence? If that was the case, I could leave now.

Too exhausted for diplomacy, I said, "Did I do something wrong?"

He spared me a disgusted glance. "I don't like it when my date looks at other men."

Okay. How to respond to that?

"I'm sorry if it seemed that way, but I assure you I'm not looking for anyone else." I wasn't even looking for *him*, technically speaking. "I really would like to hear about your writing."

To my relief, Chad's expression softened, and he shifted his chair back around. "My apologies. I shouldn't judge you by the women in my past. It's just a sore spot for me." Understandable, considering I had a similar experience the night before. He straightened his napkin and said, "I write short stories, mostly, but I've been working on a novel for five years. A little more polish and I'll be ready to look for an agent."

Five years seemed like a long time, but I'd never tried writing a novel and couldn't imagine it was easy.

"Have you had any stories published?" I asked.

The smile dimmed again and his left eye twitched. "No," he said. "Not yet. It isn't that easy. There's a lot of competition and not a lot of places print short stories anymore."

How many sore spots did this guy have? That was two in a matter of seconds.

"So… Georgetown? What was that like?"

"Good for the two years I got to go. A family issue came up and I had to quit before my junior year."

Megan said he'd graduated. Why were my friends so bad at telling me anything about these men? The first date had been nursing a broken heart. The second clearly had a thing against women who didn't drink. So far, Chad had jealousy issues—which totally explained that Darcy forgiveness thing—and multiple sensitive topics.

His attention returned to the game and this time I felt no need to earn it back. More and more locals filled the patio, raising the volume enough to make talking difficult anyway. I'd eat my grilled cheese sandwich, leave a ten on the table to cover my half, and make the short walk to my parents' house before the end of the first period.

CHAPTER NINE

NOT FAR INTO THE GAME, THE CROWD OF SPECTATORS turned angry and Chad joined in, spewing rapid-fire expletives in response to the refs putting one of our players into the penalty box. I didn't see the play, but the fans obviously considered it a bad call. To be fair, hockey fans in general believed all calls against their own team were bogus. And in many cases, they were. Just recently a ref had been caught on a hot microphone admitting as much.

"These refs suck," Chad declared, and earned a high five from two men a table over.

So he got to fraternize with our neighbors, but I couldn't even look around. Sure. Totally fair.

If I had better company this would have actually been fun. I hadn't seen a game in weeks. Dad would have it on, and I was looking forward to watching the rest with him, which made me think of the mystery box. What could be in there? I hadn't occupied that room since leaving for college nearly twelve years ago, at which point Mom had turned it into a guest room.

No telling what I'd find. Probably some embarrassing artwork from elementary school. Or a diary filled with overly dramatic stories like the time I had a crush on Johnny Cukowski in sixth grade but he'd barely acknowledged my existence.

The waiter delivered our drinks but my date was too distracted to notice. "Thank you," I said with an apologetic smile.

"You're welcome," he replied. "Your food should be up shortly."

As I reached for my glass, Chad shouted, "Pass the damn puck!" Slamming his hand on the table, he bolted from his chair and the combination knocked over my Sprite.

Shoving my chair back while simultaneously righting the drink, I managed not to wear the whole thing, but a splash of clear liquid quickly soaked through the denim covering my left thigh.

"What happened?" my date asked, his brow furrowed as if angry that I was distracting him from the game.

"You knocked over my pop," I replied, beyond annoyed. "I need to put some water on this."

Rising, I grabbed my purse and charged off toward the ladies' room, hoping I could clean the sticky mess without making things worse. Rigby's grilled cheese was one of my favorite sandwiches, but it was not good enough to endure any more of this date. I'd scrub the soda out of my pants, return to the table to let Chad know I was leaving, and then see myself out.

When I entered the restroom, two women were lingering near the sinks at the far end.

"I can't believe he has the nerve to bring a woman here," the redhead said as she leaned close to the mirror to freshen up her mascara. "He knows Jackie works every Friday night."

The second woman applied bright-pink lipstick before smacking her lips together. "He's trying to make her jealous. When is he going to get it through his thick skull that she's happy with Greg?"

"Probably never. I almost feel bad for his date. She looks nice enough. Tiny and a bit desperate, but nice."

I stepped up to the first sink, lifted my bag higher onto my shoulder, and pulled several paper towels from the dispenser. After soaking them in cold water, I dabbed at my jeans, eventually noticing an odd silence. Feeling as if I was being watched, I looked up to find the women staring with a combination of curiosity and pity in their eyes.

"It's Sprite," I said, sounding like the dork that I was.

"About before—" pink lipstick said, but her friend cut her off.

"Did he even tell you his ex works here?"

Stopping mid-dab, I opened my mouth to tell them they must have me confused with someone else, but then the truth dawned. *I* was the tiny and desperate-looking one, and that meant Chad was the one trying to make this Jackie person jealous. Oh, the irony.

Wait. I looked desperate?

"This is a blind date," I explained. "I don't know anything about an ex."

"Girl," the redhead said, crossing her arms and kicking out a hip, "get out now. That man is a mess. Jackie dated him for three months and every time she didn't answer his call or text within seconds, he accused her of being with another man. She dumped him six months ago and he's still trying to get her back."

I'd already planned to leave so the warning was unnecessary, but I thanked them anyway. "I appreciate the heads-up. I won't be staying much longer."

"Then he's already shown his ass?" she asked, chestnut brow arched.

"Something like that." I returned to cleaning my pants and the ladies left the room.

As if someone flipped a switch, my energy drained and I braced my hands on the sink to stay upright. Exhaustion hit like a weighted blanket and it took several deep breaths to keep the tears at bay. Why would I cry over a jealous idiot and some spilled Sprite?

Because this wasn't about either of those things.

My boss was dealing with cancer; I was dealing with

a workload no human being could manage, and my friends were trying to top each other in finding me the absolute worst dates ever. Dates I didn't even want to go on.

An older waitress in a green apron pushed through the door and stopped halfway to the stalls. "Are you okay, honey?"

Sniffling, I put on my best fake smile. "I'm fine, thanks."

I couldn't even be honest with a stranger. Hell, when was the last time I was honest with myself?

"You sure?" she asked again. "You look a bit pale."

I tossed the paper towels in the trash and pinched my cheeks to add color. "It's just been a long week," I explained. An understatement of epic proportions. "I'll be okay."

Would I? Not if I went on another one of these dates. Whether Lindsey's pick backed out or not, tomorrow night was not going to happen. At some point, I had to put my sanity first. Something I should have done long before now.

"All right, darling. Just be careful when you head out. The crowd is rowdier than usual tonight."

"I will, thank you."

Shifting away from the sink, I lifted my left leg and turned on the hand dryer in an effort to minimize the wet spot. Luckily, my jeans were dark so the area blended in well enough that I wouldn't be embarrassed to leave the bathroom. Hugging my purse against my side, I stepped out to a barrage of groans and heard the television announcer say, “The shot went wide but the Penguins retain possession.”

Though the path to the bathroom had been clear on my way in, the way was almost completely blocked now. I squeezed through and when I could finally see my table, the crowd erupted as I heard the telltale siren that signaled a goal had been scored. Shoved back and forth like a pinball, I felt myself losing my balance at the same moment a body slammed into me from the left. I went flying and as I landed on my bottom in a stranger’s lap, my elbow hit the table, sending pain shooting up my arm. Tucking the arm against my side, my shoulder connected with the stranger’s chin.

Mortified, I turned to apologize and found familiar brown eyes staring into mine. Panic sent my heart racing as I leaped to my feet and felt the blood rush from my head. When the black spots entered the edge of my vision, I knew what was coming next but was powerless to stop it.

I managed to say, “Not you,” before the world went black.

I HAD a sense of chaos surrounding me before realizing that I was moving. Except I wasn’t walking. At least I didn't think so. I was floating. No, someone was carrying me. Someone solid who smelled like vanilla and pine. I eased my eyes open to see silver ductwork and a polished wood ceiling before the scenery changed and the night sky filled my vision, black with tiny dots like distant fireflies.

"What are you doing?" a man demanded. "That's my date."

The whiny plea brought me back to reality. I groaned as pain echoed from several parts of my body. My left elbow. My right knee. The back of my head.

"Easy now," said a soothing voice. My bottom made contact with a flat surface. "Take your time."

Struggling to focus, I blinked until Jacob's face became clear in front of mine. His hands cupped my cheeks as if he feared my head would roll off my shoulders.

"Get your hands off her."

My rescuer ignored the command. "Do you know where you are?" he asked, eyes locked on mine.

I gave a slight nod and said, "Rigby's." Pushing his hands away, I sat up straighter and felt a twinge in my neck. My hand shot to the back of my head as I muttered an expletive.

"Let me see," Jacob said, checking beneath my hand. "You're probably going to have another bump."

These damn dates were going to leave me with a concussion yet. All the more reason to skip the next one.

At the rate I was going, the odds of me falling off the damn boat were ridiculously high.

"*Another* bump?" Chad repeated. "So you *do* know each other."

"We do," Jacob replied. "Go get her some ice."

"Screw you," my date countered. To me, he said, "The next time you want to make a guy jealous, pick someone else."

"I didn't pick you, you jerk. And you're the one trying to win back an old girlfriend."

Defending myself only made the pain worse, and I whimpered as I leaned forward, tucking my head into my lap. Tears threatened again as humiliation mixed with fatigue, and in seconds I would be in the fetal position under this chair.

Jacob rubbed my back. "Just breathe." Chest hitching, I followed the order and eventually sat up again. "Here you go," he said, handing me a napkin that came from who knew where. The kind gesture only heightened the mortification.

"I'm not usually this unstable," I said, drying my damp cheeks. "I just didn't eat much today." In truth, I hadn't eaten much all week. Who had time? Mind clearing, I dropped my hands into my lap. "What are you doing here?"

Pulling over a chair from the next table, he took a seat. "I was watching the game."

"But why *here*? Why are you always around at the worst times?"

With a half grin, he shrugged. "Lucky, I guess. Though I agree with you now. This is getting weird."

Weird didn't begin to describe these encounters.

"I won't keep you from the game," I said. "You should get back to your friends."

"How are you getting home?"

"I'm not. At least not for a while. My parents live close by. I plan to walk over there." I rose and took a second to make sure my legs were steady. Jacob stood as well, clearly prepared to catch me if necessary. I appreciated his dedication to playing the hero, but hated how weak I must have seemed.

"I'll walk with you."

Despite how attractive I found him, and how much I'd enjoyed our last conversation, all I wanted in that moment was to wallow in my self-pity alone.

"You don't have to do that."

"A minute ago you were unconscious," he reminded me. "I'd be an asshole to let you walk off alone."

Though I felt fine now, he did have a point. Mom and Dad didn't live far so it wasn't as if I'd have to endure his company for long. I'd just send him on his way before getting all the way to the door. Mom would have a field day if I showed up with a man in tow. She hadn't outright asked about my love life—or the lack thereof—but she still hinted about grandchildren now and then. Joey and

Paula had been dating for over a year, but neither were in a hurry to get married, nor were they kid people. That left me as Mom's only hope.

She was going to be sadly disappointed.

"Are you sure?" I asked. The crowd inside erupted once again. "You're going to miss a big chunk of the game."

"I'll catch the highlights later."

"What about your friends?"

He pulled out his phone, fired off a text, and dropped the cell back into his pocket. "Done. You ready?"

Was I ready to get this night over with? I sure as hell was.

Less than a minute later, we crossed East Main to Robert Avenue in companionable silence. That could have been because we'd done this—in a car—twice already, but even Tuesday night, after the first date, being alone with Jacob had felt natural. There was a calmness about him that put me at ease. He likely had the same effect on everyone he met.

I made it a full block before curiosity got the best of me. "Of all the bars in town, how did you end up at Rigby's?"

He stepped to the left to allow a woman and her dog to pass between us. "I don't live far from here. My neighbor watches games up there all the time. He invited me and since I had the night off, I decided to join him. How about you?"

"My date picked it, but I grew up around here so I know the place well. You live in Carnegie?"

"I do." We traveled another half block before he said, "Are you shooting for some blind date record?"

A fair question. Three men in four days, and for all he knew I could have gone out with someone else on the one night our paths didn't cross.

"Do you ever do something you absolutely don't want to do, but you know it'll make someone else happy so you give in?"

"Not an answer," he replied as I motioned to make a right at Washington Avenue. As we rounded the corner, he switched sides and I realized he was keeping himself between me and the passing cars. A display of chivalry I hadn't seen in years.

"Well, that's what I do," I confessed, continuing to ignore his original question. "I am physically incapable of saying the word *no*."

"I don't know. You told that jerk last night that you weren't going with him."

"That was an extreme case." I shuffled around a light post. "I never should have agreed to these dates in the first place."

We made the left onto Academy. "Then you aren't looking for love like you said?"

"Not in the least," I confessed, "but my friends refuse to accept my choice to be alone, so here I am."

He remained silent for several seconds before stopping and turning my way. "Do the guys on these dates know you aren't serious?"

An odd question. "My friends don't even know."

For the first time in our brief acquaintance, Jacob appeared agitated. "So the guys think these are real dates, and you don't have any qualms about manipulating people like that?"

"Who am I manipulating? Under the best of circumstances, most first dates never result in a second. I'm not lying to them about who I am. I'm not catfishing anyone. I simply know before I show up that nothing more will come of it. No one is getting hurt in this scenario."

His jaw twitched as he watched me with a cold glare. "You're wasting their time."

So now he was defender and protector of his entire gender?

"No," I argued, "I met a few men for what should have been a simple meal. Everyone has to eat. What's the difference if they eat with me or with someone else or eat alone? It's an hour of their lives, and as *you* well know, I've done nothing to lead any of them on. Hell, the first was in love with someone else, the second was a racist caveman, and the one you just met accused me of looking at other men before we'd even ordered our drinks. These are not victims who walked away from our dates believing they'd just met the love of their lives. If anyone has suffered from this endeavor, it's me."

"You're playing with people's feelings either way."

Hitting me where it counted, he added, “And you aren’t even being honest with your friends.”

No, I wasn’t. I hadn’t been honest with anyone, including myself, for longer than I cared to admit, but I would not have my life scrutinized and judged by a virtual stranger.

“I don’t have to defend myself to you just because you have some hero complex and got unlucky enough to stumble into my life at a few less-than-stellar moments. You can stop playing the hero now. I can take care of myself.”

He shook his head. “You passed out less than ten minutes ago. Last night you had a drink poured over your head. Before that you tried to carry a drunk man who probably outweighed you by at least fifty pounds before colliding with a tree. Is that what you call taking care of yourself?”

Having a litany of my week summed up so concisely was not what I needed right now. Anger made my cheeks hot and brought tears to my eyes. I would not add to the humiliation he’d already witnessed by letting this man see me cry.

“Do us both a favor and go save someone else.” Charging down the sidewalk, I kept my shoulders back and my chin up, pretending the world wasn’t blurring before me. I half expected him to barrel down on me, determined to fulfill his savior role or just to continue pointing out all the ways I was a shitty human being. To my relief, he let me go without another word, and I picked up my pace once I crossed the next intersection.

Jacob's accusations played over and over again in my head. I was *not* manipulating anyone. If anything, I was letting my friends manipulate me into these stupid dates. And then there was Amanda exploiting my spinelessness and dropping more work on me than I could or should have to do. Also, she hadn't even hinted at paying me more to do twice the work, and it never occurred to me to ask. Because cancer trumps fair pay, apparently. At least in my feeble, don't-rock-the-boat brain.

Around the corner from my parents' house, my frustration, anger, and suffocating helplessness poured out in a guttural scream that bent me in half. As I panted with my hands on my knees, a dog in a nearby yard barked and a woman called out of her window.

"Are you okay out there?"

I looked around and realized I was standing in the middle of the alley that ran perpendicular to my old street. Straightening, I brushed fresh tears from my cheeks and located the source of the voice. "I'm fine. Sorry I bothered you."

Taking several deep breaths, I reached the corner and turned left down Plum while pulling a tissue from my bag to blow my nose. No matter what I did, Mom would know I'd been crying. She'd always known no matter how hard I tried to hide the truth. Maybe that was the reason I hadn't visited much lately. No one else saw through me like Mom did, and she didn't need tears to know when something was wrong.

I considered ordering a car and just going home, but sometimes a girl needed her mom. This was definitely one of those times.

CHAPTER TEN

As I stepped onto the porch of the house I grew up in, memories overwhelmed me. I'd gotten good at shoving them away over the last couple of years, but in a moment of weakness—like when I'd had a terrible week and literally fainted in the last ten minutes—that was more difficult.

This was the porch where I had my first kiss. Where we took endless prom pictures. Where Brian got down on one knee and told me he'd love me forever. Closing my eyes against the onslaught, I pushed through the door and called out. "Mom? Hello?"

The petite brunette who'd given me my height—or lack thereof—my hazel eyes and my love of organization rushed into the foyer with a tea towel in hand. "Becca, honey, you're earlier than I expected. Is everything okay?"

"Dinner didn't go as planned," I said, dropping a quick kiss on her cheek.

Kathy Witherspoon was not fooled. Forcing me to make eye contact, she said, "What's wrong?"

So much. So, so much.

"Nothing. Really. Rigby's is too packed thanks to the game so I decided I'd rather watch it here. Where's that box you found?"

Eyes narrowed, she nodded toward the room on my right. "It's in the dining room. We'll take it into the kitchen so you can tell me what's going on while I finish the dishes." I'd offered to buy them a dishwasher more than once over the last few years, but Mom had brushed off the idea as if I'd suggested they get a butler. "Have you eaten?" she asked. "I can heat up some pierogi."

Never had I needed the comfort food more. "I would really like that, thanks. Dad's downstairs, right?"

The Witherspoon basement had been converted into a man cave long before the term had been invented. The only thing that had changed since I was in middle school was the size of the television.

"Of course, he is." She crossed to the door that led to the basement and yelled down, "Carl, your daughter is here."

"Send her down!" he yelled, before adding, "That was off sides!"

Mom rolled her eyes. "You can go see him after we talk. Get the box off the table while I put the food on."

I followed the order and found the mystery box heavier than expected. *Becca's stuff* was scrawled across the top in my swirly teenage handwriting, and dust filled my sinuses as I dropped it onto the kitchen table harder than I should have.

"What's going on with Aunt Jeanne?" I asked, hoping to put off the conversation I wasn't ready to have.

"Reginald has a week to move out, and then Jeanne's having some updates done to the house before putting it on the market." She pulled a skillet out of the cabinet and crossed to the fridge for butter. "I don't blame her for not wanting to be there while he's packing his things, and since we have that spare room, I told her she could stay here."

"I can't believe she's selling that house. They've been there forever."

I lifted the cardboard flaps to find my old green and gold pompoms on top of a collection of books and magazines. From third grade on, all I'd wanted was to be a cheerleader, and freshman year I finally made the team. Always the smallest on the squad, I started to rethink my choices when I found myself at the top of the pyramid three years running. By the time I graduated, I knew that cheering on the college level was not going to be for me.

"They bought the place a year before your dad and I moved in here." Mom tilted her head. "That was thirty-three years ago so, yeah, forever." When the butter started to sizzle, she tossed in the pierogi. "Now what's going on with you? And don't tell me you're fine because I know you aren't."

Of course, she did. To be fair, I hadn't been fine in a long time. This week had just pushed me past my ability to pretend.

"The girls have been setting me up on blind dates," I said, dropping the pompoms onto the table beside the box. I hadn't mentioned the dates before because of my lack of intentions. "I've had three so far this week."

Tossing the tea towel over her shoulder, she cut me a cautious glance before reaching for a spatula. "How are they going?"

"About as well as you'd expect a blind date to go, I guess. They've been awful."

I continued to go through the box as I talked. Along with several tattered copies of *Seventeen* magazine was the entire *Twilight* saga in hardback along with a slew of other angsty YA novels—which explained the weight of the box—an ancient iPod with a cracked screen, a Beyoncé CD, and *High School Musical* one, two, and three on DVD.

"Is that why you were at Rigby's?" Mom asked. "For a date?"

"Yeah." No need to mention the fainting incident. That hadn't happened since my senior year in high school when stress over possibly not getting into the same college as Brian had resulted in a lack of appetite and sleep. A period much like this week, except back then had been nothing more than adolescent drama and now my boss had cancer. “We didn’t hit it off,” I explained.

The next layer in my trip through the past was my high school yearbooks. Picking up the one from junior year, I brushed a hand across the cover and traveled back in time without having to open it. The pep rallies. The homecoming dance. The class trip to New York City when Brian told me he was going to marry me for the first time. We were at the top of the Empire State Building, and since we’d watched *Sleepless in Seattle* the week before, I assumed he was trying to be funny.

Turned out he was serious.

I dropped the yearbooks on the table as Mom said, “What was wrong with him?”

“With who?” I asked, having lost track of the conversation.

“The date.”

“Oh, yeah. He was the jealous type,” I answered as my eyes landed on my old journals. “I can’t believe I kept these.”

“Kept what?” Mom crossed to the table and looked over my shoulder. “Your diaries?”

“Journals, Mom. Not diaries.”

“What’s the difference?”

“In a diary you write Dear Diary at the top of every entry.” We’d had this same conversation when I was sixteen. “In a journal you can write anything.”

And I had. Poems, both by me and other more

talented writers. Lyrics from whatever emo song suited my emotions that day. My fears and hopes and dreams for the future. A future I'd had all mapped out with Brian and me and a house down the street filled with three perfect children and a family dog. Now the idea of a future felt as far off as a trip to Fiji.

"Here," Mom said, startling me back to the present. She patted my cheek with the towel before shoving it into my hands. "Dry your face while I clean this up."

I hadn't even realized I was crying. Annoyed that I was being such a melodramatic baby, I settled into a chair as she loaded the items back into the box. "I don't know why I'm such a mess these days. I should be fine by now."

"There's no set time for getting over a broken heart," she said. "I should have gone through this stuff myself first."

"You don't have to protect me. I'm not a baby, after all."

Closing the box, she turned and cupped my chin in her hand. "You'll always be my baby, whether you're thirteen or thirty." Gesturing to the box, she said, "I'll put this back in the closet and when you're ready, we'll pull it out again."

Nodding, I silently agreed.

Returning to the stove, she asked, "Have you not met a single nice guy on these dates?"

An interesting way to phrase it. I *had* met someone

nice. Or so I'd thought. Until he'd turned into the intention police and tried to make me feel like an asshole for going on a few harmless dates.

"No one," I said. "I don't know what the girls were thinking when they picked these men. None of them are right for me."

"Are you sure you aren't being too picky?"

Too picky was disqualifying a guy for not driving the right car. That was not the problem this week.

"Am I a jerk for agreeing to these dates without intending to take them seriously?" I asked.

Mom's lips puckered as she took several seconds to answer. "Why did you agree to them then?" she asked, and I realized where I got the *answer a question with a question* habit from.

"Then you *do* think I'm a jerk."

"I didn't say that." She flipped the pierogi before turning to lean a hip against the counter. Arms crossed, she repeated, "Why did you agree to the dates?"

I sighed. "Because the girls are worried about me and I figured going on the dates would show them that I'm fine now. They would stop worrying, and we could all get on with our lives."

Sliding the skillet onto the back burner, Mom crossed to the table and sat down. "But you aren't."

"I'm not what?" I asked.

"Fine or moving on." Mom pressed her hand over mine. "Becca, you have a long life ahead of you. Do you ever think about taking a trip or exploring a new hobby? Anything that would give you something to look forward to?"

Other than the events I planned for work, I never thought about the future. I'd had big plans once. Places I wanted to see. Things I wanted to do. And then the plan got blown to bits and I learned real quick that planning is pointless when in a split second your whole life can change.

"My job is about the future, remember? We're busier than ever and now that Amanda will be out of the office, I won't have time for trips or hobbies for a while."

"Why is she out of the office? That woman already works you to death. She doesn't expect you to do everything, does she?"

That's exactly what she expected. "This can't be helped, Mom. Amanda has cancer and she needs time off for the treatments. It's only for a few months."

"Meredith Rebecca Witherspoon, cancer is no excuse to run you into the ground," she snapped, warrior mom activated. "You've clearly lost weight, and you look like you haven't slept in days. How are you possibly going to run that place by yourself?"

Why did no one understand the words *I have no choice*?

"I've looked at the schedule and I can make it work. Marquette will handle things at the office, and he'll help out more when I need him to." After all, what Amanda didn't know wouldn't hurt her. Or get me fired, hopefully. "It's not as if she went out and got cancer to make my life more difficult. Beating this is her top priority, and I'll take care of the rest to make sure she still has a business when she comes back."

"I'm sorry that she has cancer, but I still don't like this," Mom grumbled, returning to the stove. She pulled a plate from the top cabinet and slid the pierogi from the pan. "Promise me you'll say something if it gets to be too much. And you have to start eating more. I don't like how tiny you've gotten."

Extra meals didn't fit in the schedule, but I would do my best. "I promise." Taking the plate from her hands, I said, "I'm going to eat this downstairs with Dad. Do you need me to take him anything?"

Without a word, she turned and pulled a bag of pretzels from the cabinet. As if he could smell them, we heard a voice from the distance.

"Kathy, hon, send down the pretzels."

"How did you know?" I asked.

"He took the popcorn down an hour ago." Due to cholesterol issues, Dad was supposed to stay off the snacks, but the best Mom had been able to do was switch him to healthier ones. "He averages a bag an hour so this should last through the rest of the game."

I tucked the bag under my arm and turned toward the front hall.

"I'm always here to talk," Mom said as I was heading downstairs. "You know that, right?"

Turning, I shared a genuine smile. "I do."

She nodded and went back to her dishes in the sink, but I could see the concern still etched on her face. I hated that she worried about me. It seemed as if everyone worried about me these days. I'd have to work harder to make them see that I was fine. Or mostly fine. Either way, I'd be more than happy to stop being the center of everyone's attention. I wasn't some fragile doll in need of fixing. This week was testing me, that was all.

So there'd been a few moments of weakness. Everyone had bad days. I was just having a bad week. And after this last disaster of a date, I was done with the worst part anyway. I'd let Lindsey know to cancel the dinner cruise, and after making it through the graduation party, Sunday was my day of rest. A day to sleep in, spend some quiet time on the couch with Milo, and put the last few days behind me.

By the time I reached Dad's man cave, I was already feeling better.

"Hey, pumpkin. What took you so long?" Dad asked as I handed over the pretzels. He set them on the small table beside his recliner, where he hovered on the edge, ready to leap to his feet either in celebration or disgust at any moment. "You've missed half the game."

"Mom made me some pierogi," I explained, leaving out how my evening started and the tears shed upstairs. "What's the score?"

"We're tied at one. Sid is getting slammed from every direction, and the refs aren't calling shit."

"So a typical playoff game," I muttered, digging into my meal.

The man cave hadn't changed much. The same banners—for the Steelers, Pirates, and Penguins—covered the walls. There was even one for the professional lacrosse team that had represented the city back in the early nineties.

Local colleges were represented, of course. Pitt. Duquesne. And the slightly farther away but equally supported Penn State. The neon Iron City sign Mom bought him for Christmas had been mounted over the bar in the back corner since I was last here. It shared pride of place with the Jerome Bettis signed and framed football jersey that was already there.

In the early days, the basement had truly felt like a cave, since the previous homeowners had installed dark wood paneling when they'd turned the space into a gaming room. Once Dad painted the walls yellow and cleaned up the two windows at the top of the wall where the flat screen now hung, the place had actually become bright and cheerful.

Dad cut a glance my way. "How are things with you? The job keeping you too busy to come see your old man?"

In the past, I'd made a point to visit every Sunday, but lately I was either running an event or recovering from handling several back-to-back.

"I'm sorry."

"You don't need to apologize, sweetie. That's how it goes sometimes."

"But I should make time to see you and Mom."

"Eh," he grunted. "You're young. You don't need to be hanging out with us old people."

They weren't that old. "Dad, you're only fifty-five. You still play on a softball team, run three miles every morning, and could dance circles around most twenty-year-olds."

The siren sounded from the television and he slammed a hand down on the side table, crushing the poor pretzels. "Dammit, where's the defense?"

We watched the replay together and I said, "They were blocking his view of the puck, that's where they were."

"Shit," Dad murmured. "Get it back, boys. Get it back." The game cut to a commercial and he sat back in his chair. "How are you really doing?"

Swallowing half a pierogi, I shook my head. "I'm fine."

"You know it's okay if you aren't."

Did I have poor pitiful me written across my forehead?

"But I *am* fine." *Those* were the words I should have tattooed on my forehead.

"I'm just saying, it's like that show your mom got me to watch a few months ago. The one that said it's okay to not be okay."

I froze with my fork halfway to my mouth. "You watched a Korean drama?"

He looked as if I'd caught him stealing a cookie. "I didn't plan on it but by the end of the first episode I had to know who killed their mom. Anyway," he said, leaning forward with his elbows on his knees, "if you say you're fine, then that's good. But if you aren't, that's good too."

How could it be good to not be fine?

"There's no need to worry about me, Dad. Really."

"Who said I was worried?" His attention returned to the TV as he reached for the pretzels. "Just because your eyes are swollen and your nose is red. You're obviously fine."

He always was too observant.

"I went through the box that Mom found," I said, my voice small. "The memories were a little too much." The pierogi started to taste like sandpaper so I set the plate aside. "Can I ask you something?"

"Ask away," he replied.

"Would you mind if a woman went to dinner with you even if she didn't really intend to date you?"

His lips twisted to one side. "I think your mom might have something to say about that."

"This is a hypothetical, Dad. I'm talking about when you were younger, before you met Mom. Would you have been annoyed to find out you got set up with someone and she only had dinner with you to make her friends happy?"

He looked to be taking the question seriously as he rubbed his chin. "If I took the time to go on the date, I'd be a little annoyed to find out she was never going to be interested."

Not the answer I wanted to hear.

"Why?"

"Why would I be annoyed?"

"Yes. If you got a nice meal and interesting conversation, what's the harm?"

He crossed his arms. "The harm is that I'd be wasting my time and not know it. What if I really like her? What if I think she's someone I want to spend more time with only to learn that she'd already ruled me out before we even met? That doesn't sound fair, does it?"

I hadn't thought of it that way, mostly because I hadn't expected any of these dates to actually like me. And in the end, none of them had. But what if the circumstances had been different? What if even one of them had been a nice, available guy who'd assumed the same about me? Then I'd have been a pretty shitty person for agreeing to do this without ever intending to give him a chance.

"Then it's better to not go on the date at all," I decided.

"Maybe," he said, pouring a handful of pretzels. "Or you could go on the date with an open mind and see how things go."

Meeting his eyes, I said, "This is just a hypothetical situation, remember?"

Dad nodded. "Sure, it is. I'm just saying that you could, hypothetically speaking, give the guy a chance."

I could. But did I want to? No matter how the first three dates had gone, I didn't exactly look like the good guy in this scenario. Instead of canceling the last one, I could take it seriously and see what happened. I still didn't think anything more than a nice dinner would come out of it, but at least I'd redeem myself in my own mind. And fulfill the promise I made during the group chat.

"I'll think about it," I said, before realizing I'd uttered the words aloud. With a noncommittal shrug, I added, "Hypothetically."

Dad had the nerve to laugh.

CHAPTER ELEVEN

AFTER CAREFUL CONSIDERATION, AN IN-DEPTH DISCUSSION with Milo—during which I'd done most of the talking—plus a night of little sleep, I decided to take Dad's advice. Not only would I keep this last date, but I would go into it without prejudice. No preconceived notions. No bad intentions.

This did not, however, mean that I was suddenly being optimistic. The chances were still slim that I would make a romantic connection, but at least I would be able to walk away from the date—preferably with no further injuries—knowing I hadn't wasted anyone's time. And though it was highly unlikely I would run into my holier-than-thou rescuer on a boat floating down the Monongahela… Or would we be on the Allegheny? Whichever river this boat took, there would be no Jacob encounter, but I would still know that *if* he showed up again, he would have no reason to judge me this time.

And so I started the day feeling pretty positive. Then I reached the banquet hall for the graduation party and positive went out the window. Though Amanda and I were the only planners at the company, that did not mean we did the physical labor ourselves. There were two teams of setup staff that we used for our events. They did the load-in, hung the decorations, and handled breakdown and cleanup at the end. They were also our eyes and ears in many cases, since it was simply impossible to be everywhere at once.

Monique's crew was on duty for the graduation party and had started the tedious task of blowing up balloons and hanging streamers nearly an hour before I arrived. The place was decked out in black and red—for the graduate's school colors—and had been placed exactly to the client's instructions. Having the crew take care of the details meant I could focus on the client, which was one of the biggest selling points of Three Rivers Events. We were always available when they needed us.

The outside vendors were the problem today. First, the DJ tripped a breaker, which required contacting hall maintenance. Nearly thirty minutes later, an older gentleman finally arrived with a key to access the breaker box. Cords were rearranged to even out the outlet usage and the music was once again up and running.

Then the caterer showed up nearly forty minutes late.

After I left four frantic messages, they finally strolled in, delayed because of a flat tire on the way. It was at that point I realized this was going to be one of *those* days when what could go wrong would, and I'd just have to be ready when it did.

However, to my shock and utter amazement, there were no more problems. The caterer had plenty of food, which the guests loved, and the buffet ran like a dream. The PA system worked without a hitch and the graduate's father gave a speech that brought the entire room to tears. Thankfully, the napkins were still on the tables, and many were covered in mascara stains by the time he finished. The lady of the hour also gave a speech, this one less tearful but just as heartfelt.

She thanked her parents, her friends, and last but not least, her boyfriend of three years who, she claimed had gotten her through high school without losing her mind or flunking out of calculus. They were both moving on to Penn State in the fall, which explained the extra blue and silver balloons requested for the main table.

Though this reminded me of my own high school days—and my excitement about also attending Penn State with Brian—my emotions did not get away from me like they had the day before. A sure sign that the crying jag had been a moment of weakness brought on by a stressful week and nothing more.

At the two-hour mark, I felt confident that I could leave the partygoers on their own. The last hour was left for dancing and dessert, neither of which required my supervision. After making one last check with the DJ, the caterer, and the graduate's parents, I was ready to order a car but was cut off on my way to the exit.

"Becca Witherspoon?"

I spun to see a familiar face to which I struggled to put a name. "Yes?" I said, hoping the person would refresh my memory.

"It's me," said the willowy brunette with big brown eyes and a wide smile. "Pepper Romano. I haven't seen you since the reunion."

How could I forget Pepper? We hadn't run in the same circles back in high school, but she'd been like the human mascot for our class with more energy than that drumming pink bunny, and enough positivity to make even the most jaded of students experience an unwelcome hit of optimism. I'd often braced when I saw her coming, but her bubbly nature made it impossible not to like her.

The reunion she referenced had taken place mere weeks before my life had changed.

"Of course, I know it's you," I said. "Do you know the graduate?"

She nodded. "She's my fiancé's cousin. I don't know her that well, but she seems sweet."

"She is," I confirmed. When we planned high school graduations, the parents normally took charge, but not in this case. Amanda had commented that her encounters with Gabby had been more professional than many she had with adults. "So you're engaged?"

Pepper flashed an impressive rock on her left hand. "Since Christmas. Oh, I should call you about planning it for us. Jackson wants to finish his residency before we pick a date." She shimmied with excitement. "I still can't believe I'm marrying a doctor. Holding off on the planning has practically killed me."

"Well, I'd be happy to help you out. That is what we do." I pulled a business card from my pocket. It was important to always have them on hand during an event for just such encounters. "It's never too early to start planning." I remembered Amanda's declaration that we were closed to new clients. "Let me give you my cell so you can call me directly." I flipped the card and wrote my number on the back before handing it over.

"That's so sweet of you," she said. "So how have you been?"

"Good. Business is a little crazy right now, going into the height of wedding season, and graduations, of course."

"But how are *you*?" she emphasized. "Are you seeing anyone? Not that anyone would blame you if you aren't. After what happened..."

The pity in her eyes made me feel two inches tall.

"I'm fine. Really. I'm not seeing anyone exclusively, but I am dating." A statement that would not have been true before this week, but Pepper didn't need to know that. "Not every girl can be lucky enough to find a doctor, after all. Some of us have to search a little harder to find Mr. Right."

I was starting to nauseate myself with this dribble. There was a reason I hated small talk. Mostly because I sucked at it. Add defensiveness to the mix, and I became the person I never wanted to be.

"He's out there," she assured me. "But you shouldn't feel rushed. After what hap—"

"I'd really like to stay and catch up," I cut in, "but I have another event to get to, so I really need to go. Call my cell whenever you're ready to start looking at venues, okay? We'll catch up more then."

Rushing through the door before she could respond, I stood beneath a weathered green awning and watched a steady drizzle soak everything in sight. Worried she might come out to find me lingering about, I took a few seconds to order a car before pulling an umbrella from my bag and moving farther down the building to the corner to wait. Thankfully, the driver was only a few minutes away.

That was just long enough for Pepper's words to play over and over in my mind. Was that what everyone thought? Poor Becca? Yes, what happened two years ago sucked. It sucked a lot. But the last thing I wanted was to be pitied. I had a life. A satisfying one. Not wanting to date didn't mean I was some sad spinster that people should feel sorry for.

As my ride pulled up, I grew even more determined to make the most of this last date. I'd show everyone. Poor, pitiful Becca was absolutely fine. Better than fine. She was ready to move on. In fact, this guy was about to have the best date of his life. Better than any date he'd ever had. I'd show them. I'd show them all.

"I'M TELLING YOU, Megan, I have nothing to wear."

My friend's gaze shifted from the bed, which was covered in no less than ten dresses, to the closet and back to me. "You have a million things to wear. Why are you freaking out? This isn't like you."

Frustrated, I tossed another dress onto the pile and the hanger smacked Milo in the head, causing him to bolt out of the room with an angry snarl. "Sorry, buddy." To Megan I said, "This is my first date in years, and I want to make a good impression."

Blinking, she crossed her arms and leaned against my dresser. "You've had *three* other dates just this week. Did you forget about those?"

Shoot. Me and my big mouth. "I—"

"Come to think of it, I don't recall you being this nervous or meticulous about any of those. You haven't been taking these seriously, have you?"

Why hadn't I thought of this before calling her over?

"Maybe I didn't give my best effort, but—"

"But what?" she cut in. "Did those dates really go as badly as you said?"

She couldn't really think I made all that up. "I have been completely honest about every minute of those dates. They were horrible, and I have the bruising and liquor-stained clothing to prove it. But I'm taking *this one* seriously, and I didn't call you over here to interrogate me." Dragging two more dresses from the closet, I held them up in front of me. "What about these ones?"

"The yellow," she said without hesitation.

Looking at the frilly number, I said, "Really?"

"Yes. Yellow looks amazing on you, and that dress is the prettiest thing you own. Now tell me why."

"Why what?" I asked as she carried dresses from the bed back to the closet.

"Why *this* guy? You obviously wrote off the rest of our picks, so why is Lindsey's worth all of this fuss?"

How did I explain that I was trying to prove a point to a total stranger that I would never see again? Not that Jacob's reaction was the only reason I was doing this. The talk with Dad had changed my view on a few things, especially when he'd echoed Jacob's statement about wasting the other person's time. Then there'd been Pepper's pity party that sent me over the edge.

Maybe all of this was the universe's way of telling me I was ready to try again.

"Do you know the story of how Brian and I met?" I asked.

"In high school," she said. "We all know that."

"I mean *how* we met in high school." I dropped onto the stool in front of my vanity. "It was Lindsey. She sat next to him in homeroom sophomore year and insisted that he was the perfect guy for me."

Megan's eyes went wide. "How did I not know that?"

Shrugging, I said, "It never came up, I guess. I'm not delusional enough to think this date is going to turn into my happily ever after. I just want to remember what it feels like to be out with a guy and have a nice time. Maybe it won't go any better than the first three, but I'll know that this time I gave it my best shot."

Milo jumped up on the vanity and headbutted my shoulder as Megan said, "What if this guy *does* turn out to be the one?"

The response in my brain was loud and instantaneous. *I already found the one*. But maybe there was a different *the one* out there somewhere. Who was to say I couldn't love someone else? It wouldn't be the same, but different didn't necessarily mean it couldn't be just as good.

"Stranger things have happened." I rubbed Milo's chin. "He'll have to like cats though, right, buddy? You and me are a package deal."

Megan snorted. "Good luck getting Milo to share you with anyone. Now let's get you dressed. What time are you meeting this guy?"

"Six o'clock on the Clipper for a dinner cruise." I

checked the time on my phone. “Crap. I have less than an hour.”

Scrambling into the bathroom, I dragged my makeup bag out from under the sink. I couldn’t remember the last time I wore more than a little mascara and some lip gloss.

“What’s his name, anyway?” Megan asked as she took a seat on the side of the tub.

I stopped fishing around for my favorite lipstick and stood up straight, catching my blank stare in the mirror. “I have no idea.”

“You forgot his name?”

“No, she never told me.” Dashing back into the bedroom, I grabbed my phone and dialed Lindsey’s number. After five rings I got her voicemail. Ending the call, I immediately tried again, and again she didn’t answer.

“Let me try,” Megan said, making the call on her own cell. Seconds later she pulled the phone away from her ear. “She isn’t answering for me either.”

I fired off an all caps text.

WHERE THE HECK ARE YOU? I NEED TO KNOW THIS GUY’S NAME!

Staring at the screen, I willed her to answer when Megan’s phone started to ring. “It’s Donna,” she said as I looked up expectantly. Answering, she said, “Hey, lady, what’s up?”

I went back to staring at my phone. How was I supposed to meet a total stranger in less than an hour without knowing his name or what he looked like. I couldn't ask every man who went near the boat if he was my date. I'd look like a crazy woman.

"Wait, is Lindsey with you?" Megan said. A second passed before she added, "Becca needs the info on her date."

"Let me talk to her," I said, reaching for the phone.

Megan shook her head. "They're at dinner and Lindsey's in the bathroom. She left her phone on the table." Going back to the call, she said, "Becca meets this guy in less than an hour and she doesn't even know his name. Tell Lindsey to call her when she comes back." Waving a hand in my direction, she whispered, "We'll get the details. Just hold on."

Knowing I'd have to order a car soon, I said, "Put her on speaker so I can talk to her while doing my makeup."

We returned to our positions in the bathroom and I frantically applied foundation as Donna conveyed the message to Lindsey.

"I sent it all in an email," I heard Lindsey say.

"When?" I said as Megan held her phone beside my head.

"A few hours ago. His name is Jacob Kim. You shouldn't have any trouble spotting him. He looks like those guys in the dramas you love. Tall, thick dark hair, broad shoulders, and he even has dimples. All the other details are in the email."

I dropped the blending sponge into the sink as my

heart slammed against my chest. “What did she say?” I whispered.

“What’s wrong?” Megan asked, concern creasing her brow. “You look like you’ve seen a ghost.”

“What was that?” Lindsey said. “I can’t hear you.”

This couldn’t really be possible. I had no idea what Jacob’s last name was, but Kim certainly fit. And Lindsey had echoed my exact same thought about him strolling out of a drama. Maybe this was just a coincidence. I mean, what were the odds that *this* Jacob would be *my* Jacob.

My Jacob? Where did that come from?

“Are you guys still there?” Lindsey said.

“Hold on,” Megan replied. Sensing my panic, she said, “We’ll call you back in a minute.”

After ending the call, she took me by the shoulders and sat me down on the toilet seat. “Why do you look like you’re about to pass out? Becca, do you know this guy already?”

Did I? I wanted so badly to say no but every bone in body said that would be a lie.

“There’s been this guy…” I started.

“What guy? Did someone hurt you?”

“No! Nothing like that.” I dropped my eyes to the tiny black and white tiles beneath my feet. “The same stranger has popped up on each of the dates. The first night he was the driver who picked us up and eventually brought me home after I hit my head. The next night he was the bouncer who kicked my date out of the bar. Then last night, he just happened to be watching the game at Rigby's and caught me when I fainted."

"You fainted?"

I really had been holding out on them. "I did, but I'm fine. Megan, that stranger's name is Jacob. I don't know what his last name is, but he's Asian and fits Lindsey's description exactly. What if he's the date?"

"Then it isn't a blind date after all. What's the problem? Is he a jerk or something?"

No, *I* was the jerk. And he knew it. "I told him I was only going on these dates to get you guys to leave me alone. He knows I wasn't taking them seriously."

Megan cringed. "So he'll think you aren't taking this one seriously either."

"Exactly." Lifting my gaze to meet hers, I confessed the most crucial part. "It gets worse."

She dropped onto the side of the tub. "How much worse?"

Shoulders dropping, I admitted the truth. "I like him. I really like him."

Popping up like the cheerleader she once was, Megan jerked me to my feet. "Then we have to get you ready. Move, woman. You've got a man to meet."

She wasn't getting this. "You're missing the point, Meg. The minute he sees me, he's going to turn around and leave. He was pissed when I told him what I was doing. There's no way he's going to stick around long enough for me to convince him that this time is different."

"Then you have to make him listen. Hon, you haven't even hinted at liking anyone since Brian. This guy *must* be special, and if the universe is throwing you together like this, then it's meant to be." She shook with excitement. "This is your guy. You have to do this."

"How?" I said. I couldn't exactly tackle him. How was I going to force him to hear me out?

Megan rubbed her forehead while pacing the small area, and then suddenly yelled, "Ah ha!"

I'd never seen such a diabolical look on her face. "What?"

"The boat."

"The Clipper?"

"Yes. Make him meet you *on* the boat, but don't let him find you until you've already set sail. Then he can't leave. Not without jumping overboard and there's no way he's going to do that."

The way things were going there was always the chance *I* would be the one to go overboard. I'd just have to stay away from the railings and hope my luck had changed.

"I like this idea, but how? If he expects to meet me on the dock and I don't show, he'll think he's been stood up and leave."

Determined, Megan again paced like a detective on

the verge of solving a case. "Let's see what the email says."

Oh, right. The email. I pulled up the app on my phone and found the message from two hours ago.

"Here it is," I said. "Lindsey told him to meet me on the top deck. Board time is five forty-five and the boat pulls out at six." The next sentence made my heart drop. "She included his cell number and says she gave him mine."

"Perfect. You message him to keep him on the boat until it pulls out, then surprise him."

"Maybe," I muttered, uncertain how this was going to work. He may not be able to get out of taking the cruise, but that didn't mean he had to spend it with me.

"Wait," Megan said, "Lindsey must have told him your name. Doesn't that mean he already knows it's you?"

I hadn't thought of that. We never exchanged last names, so maybe I was safe. Then I remembered the night we met.

"Oh, no."

"What?"

"He thinks my name is Meredith."

With a head tilt, she said, "Your name is Meredith, but how would he know that? You never use it."

I sighed. "It's the name I have in the app where I order cars. Since it's the name on my credit card, it's easier to use it for stuff like that."

"Okay. Why is this an oh no thing then? Lindsey surely told him your name is Becca so he's still in the dark. He has no reason not to show up."

"True, but he'll think I gave him a fake name. That means not only do I lure men out on dates while wanting nothing to do with them, but I also lie about who I am." Dropping my head into my hands, I moaned in defeat. "He's never going to want anything to do with me."

Megan sat down on the tub again and forced me to sit up. "You can do this. Once you're on the boat, you explain everything. The name. The date stuff. Tell him all of it, especially the part about you really liking him. If he's as great as Lindsey says, then he'll understand. And if he's still a jerk, then he wasn't the guy for you, but you'll have taken a step in the right direction. You'll have put yourself out there again. That's important, Becca. That's a big deal."

I wanted to believe it could be that simple, but he had no reason to give me even a minute to explain. He knew too much, and what he didn't know didn't make me look any better. Still, she had a point. I'd shut down two years ago, and I never thought that would change. Before this week, I was totally prepared to never try again. Until a kind man with beautiful brown eyes and heart-stopping dimples walked into my life and woke something inside of me.

Something I'd thought was long gone.

"I'll give it a try," I said, rising to my feet. "What's the worst that can happen?"

"Good Lord, woman," Megan snapped with a stern expression. "After the week you've had, don't even go there. Hurry up and get the dress on so we can get you dolled up and out of here. The last thing we need is for you to miss that boat."

Jumping into action, I rushed into my room to change, sending up a silent prayer to whatever higher power had been tossing this man into my life. There had to be a reason, and even if all that came out of this night was a chance to redeem myself in his eyes, that would be enough.

CHAPTER TWELVE

I LITERALLY LIVED FIVE MINUTES FROM WHERE THE Clipper docked, which was the only reason I made the boat on time. Megan had called Lindsey back to get a few more details about Jacob while I applied makeup at warp speed. I was ninety-nine percent sure that the man I was about to meet was the same man I'd been running into all week, but that one percent was enough to make me ask a few more questions.

Of course, we had to do so in such a way that would not reveal *why* we were asking. I still didn't want Lindsey to know that I might already be acquainted with her pick. For one, she'd likely be pissed, and maybe a little hurt, that I hadn't mentioned him before. And for two, there was still a slim chance that this was all a giant coincidence and Jacob Kim had never laid eyes on me before.

If that was the case, I had no idea what my reaction

would be. I'd already decided to go into the date with good intentions, and if this man really was a total stranger, then my encounters with the other Jacob were just a fluke and our paths were unlikely to ever cross again.

The first task was for Megan to find out if he had other jobs. After dancing around the topic, she determined that Lindsey believed teaching was his only occupation. That would obviously mean this wasn't my Jacob, but I floated back to the night he drove me home from the North Shore. He'd said he had one more job, but dodged the question about what that job was. I couldn't fathom why but maybe his moonlighting wasn't something he shared with his fellow teachers.

Other questions had been about his height, his features, his voice, and his history. The last wouldn't help me determine the viability of him being my rescuer, but we had to throw in something to keep Lindsey from growing suspicious. The only thing she knew was that he'd been in the area for the last eight years and he was divorced. The last made me more curious than anything. I wouldn't dare to bring up the subject, but that didn't mean I wasn't dying to know who would leave such a kind, generous, mild-mannered guy.

Or maybe he left her. Oh, what if she cheated on him? That would probably make him super sensitive to lying. Another strike against me having any chance to explain.

Primping until the last second, I walked out of the building the same moment the car pulled up to get me.

"You're all gussied up," said my driver, a friendly older man named Hank. "Got a lucky fella waiting for ya?" Before I could answer, he added, "Or a pretty girl. I'm all for that love is love stuff."

"I do have a date, yes." I tried to smile but it was difficult with my heart racing like it was. "It's a blind date," I added, unsure why I would tell a stranger such a thing.

"I didn't think you kids did that anymore. I met my Debra on a blind date. Turned out we'd worked together at a grocery store a few years before, so it wasn't as blind as either of us expected."

He had my attention. "Then you liked each other already?"

He shook with laughter as if I'd cracked a great joke. "Heavens, no. She hated me. Said I was always chasing different girls." Sharing a wink in the mirror, he said, "She was right, but I won her over."

Trying to scoot forward in my seat, I nearly choked myself with the seat belt. "How did you do it?" I asked, not above taking advice anywhere I could get it.

"Ah, I like to think I charmed her, but the truth is I just wore her down. I knew she was the girl for me. Knew it five minutes into the date." He met my eye again. "That's how it happens sometimes. Don't let anyone tell you different. We been married thirty-four years come this October, and there ain't a day I'm not grateful to my cousin Judy for setting us up."

Wearing Jacob down wasn't the best plan, but it was better than anything I'd come up with in the last hour. I could always follow him around the boat until he either agreed to listen or hid in the men's room. He didn't seem like the hiding type, but then I'd never considered myself the crazy type, yet this plan was sounding crazier by the second.

Hank pulled the car to a stop in front of the long walkway that led down to the dock. "Here you go, darling. I hope you have as much luck as I did."

"Me too," I said, but my hopes were not high.

Before I'd left the house, Megan and I had devised a time frame, during which I'd send two texts to Jacob. The first saying I was running late but would be there before the cruise set sail. The second saying I was on the boat and trying to find him. These would go out five minutes apart.

I'd attempted to alter my appearance as much as possible so if I just kept my back to him, he might not recognize me. He'd not seen me in a frilly dress, nor with my hair pulled up. Accomplishing the latter had required a record number of bobby pins, but Megan had done an impressive job, even managing to get the perfect wispy locks to dangle around my face.

Lindsey's email had included the info needed to get on board, and after scanning the crowd, I made my way onto the boat without seeing Jacob. The upper deck was far too open to provide a hiding place so I picked a spot inside on the first level where I could see both the boarding ramp and the stairs that led to the higher decks. The plan was to wait until I saw him board before sending the first text, and as time ticked by and he didn't appear, I feared all of this spy behavior was for nothing.

If the Jacob I was meeting was someone completely different, he could have walked by already and I had no idea. At five fifty-five I fired off the first message, since if I really was meeting a stranger, he needed to know I wasn't standing him up. Palms sweaty, I hit send and went back to watching out the window. The more people boarded, the more the boat moved, forcing me to brace a hand against the wall to keep my balance.

"Dear, do you know where the restroom is?"

I turned to find an elderly woman staring expectantly over her wire-rimmed glasses. "Straight down this side and at the far end," I answered. At this point in my career, I'd planned weddings on every boat in the fleet and was well-acquainted with the layout of each. "Keep going and you can't miss it."

"Thank you," she said and shuffled off in the direction I'd pointed. At the same time, my phone dinged and I checked to find a response text from my date.

I'm on the top deck.

Crap. Either I missed him, or this Jacob truly was a stranger. Taking a deep breath, I forced myself to relax.

The odds were now in favor that I was meeting someone new and I had to reset my expectations. I reminded myself that he was still the man that Lindsey described. She was confident that we would hit it off and I had every reason to trust her judgment.

This also meant that I wasn't starting at a disadvantage. This Jacob had no reason to dislike me on sight. He didn't know that I'd been disingenuous on the previous dates, that I inelegantly ran into a tree, or that I fainted in the middle of a crowded restaurant.

After another deep breath, I felt the floor move beneath my feet and realized the boat was pulling away from the dock. Relieved, I stepped outside and made my way up the stairs to the upper deck. The wind whipped the stray locks across my face as I reached the top, and as I brushed them out of my eyes, I spotted a man standing alone at the far end. His back was to me as he stared out over the river, but when he turned to glance up at the passing skyscrapers, my heart stopped.

He wasn't a stranger after all.

"JACOB," I muttered. The word came out as a whisper and was lost on the wind.

I tried to move, to walk closer, but my feet refused to obey. As if sensing he was no longer alone, Jacob turned with a smile on his perfectly curved lips. Until he saw me and the smile disappeared.

"What are *you* doing here?" he said, his brows nearly meeting.

That's right. Why would he think I was his date? He thought he was meeting a Becca not a Meredith. It hurt that he looked so annoyed to see me, but I couldn't blame him.

Swallowing the lump in my throat, I pulled my shawl tight and stepped forward. "I'm Becca," I said.

His jaw visibly tightened as he shook his head. "Your name is Meredith."

I nodded. "It is. Meredith Rebecca Witherspoon. My friends call me Becca." Clearly annoyed, his eyes cut back to the city skyline and I could practically see his brain turning. Deciding whether to stay. Or cursing the gods for putting me in his path one more time. "I use my real name in the app because it ties to my credit card. I never meant to deceive you."

"So you know Lindsey?" he asked, ignoring my statement.

"We've been best friends since we were kids."

"Then did you tell her why you go on these dates?"

Not wanting him to think she was somehow complicit, I said, "She doesn't know that I wasn't taking them seriously. But that isn't the case this time."

"Did you know it was me?" he asked, shoving his hands into the pockets of his black dress pants. He wore a matching black suit jacket over a white button-down shirt. With the top button open and his hair slicked back off his forehead, he was the epitome of beautiful, but it was the man on the inside that I truly liked.

"I guessed, but I knew nothing about who she'd picked until an hour ago."

"And you still came? You don't want to be on these dates, and you know how I feel about what you're doing. You could have saved us both the trouble."

"Please," I said, "this date is different. I *do* want to be here."

"Why? You said you want to be alone." He crossed to the railing as if desperate to put more space between us. "You're just meeting men for dinner to get it over with, remember? Well, I'm not interested in that." Storming past me, he added, "Stand up to your friends, Mere… Becca. This isn't fair to them either."

I reached for his arm. "Jacob, please wait. Let me explain."

He brushed me off and charged down the stairs, refusing to listen. So fine, I hadn't gone into the dates wholeheartedly, but he didn't even know me. I had reasons, damn it. And he was going to hear them.

"How is what I did any different than what you're doing now?" I snapped, following him down the stairs. "Did you come on this date to try to meet someone or not?"

"I came on this date to meet the person Lindsey told me about, not you."

"But that *is* me," I argued. "It's true that I didn't want to go on those other dates, but I want to go on this one. I wanted to ask you out the night you kicked that caveman date of mine out of Marco's. I just wasn't ready then." I struggled to keep up in my strappy heels. "Would you please slow down. I'm going to break my neck on these stairs."

"What did you say?" he asked, spinning and making me nearly run into him.

Out of breath, I stopped and clung to the railing as the boat swayed. "Which part?"

"The you weren't ready part. What does that mean?"

Of course, that was the part he picked up on. I'd come here to be totally honest, but some stories were harder to tell than others.

"I was engaged," I said.

"You were engaged two nights ago?"

"No, I was engaged two years ago." The boat lurched, nearly sending me over the railing. "This is a difficult story to tell. Can we please go back up and sit down? If after hearing me out you still want to get as far away from me as humanly possible, then I'll leave you alone."

His expression didn't soften as he looked off toward downtown, which was passing by at a solid clip. "Go on up. I'll follow you."

One hurdle crossed. Now the real challenge was about to begin. I didn't talk much about what happened with Brian. I probably should have. Then maybe telling this story wouldn't feel like volunteering to have myself drawn and quartered. Once I reached the top, I took a seat on one of the navy-blue metal benches that were bolted to the floor—for obvious reasons— and scooted in to make room. Jacob took a seat at the end, leaving several feet of space between us.

Not a great sign but at least he was willing to listen.

"I was supposed to get married two years ago in June. Brian was my high school sweetheart and is still the only guy I've ever dated."

"The only guy?" he asked, brow arched. I knew what he was really asking.

"Yes," I confirmed. "The *only* guy. The day before the wedding, Brian went to the mall to pick up his tux. Do you remember what happened at the mall in Green Tree two years ago?"

Jacob started to shake his head, but then his expression softened. "The shooting."

A lump formed in my throat as I struggled to keep my emotions in check. "That's right. A lone gunman opened fire, killing eight people before turning the gun on himself. Brian was one of those eight." The tears came immediately, as they always did on the rare occasions I was forced to recall that day. Clearing my throat, I said, "Once you lose the love of your life, the idea of dating anyone else feels pretty pointless. So that's why I didn't want to go on those dates. Or any dates for that matter."

I swiped the tears away. "I couldn't imagine feeling for anyone else what I had with Brian. At the same time, I didn't want my friends to worry about me anymore. I thought if I went on the dates, they would be happy and see that I'm all right. I never wanted anyone to get hurt or to feel manipulated, but you're right, I didn't take the men's feelings into account, and I'm sorry about that."

Seconds passed in silence before he said, "That was the day before your wedding?"

"Yeah," I said, blowing out a hitched breath. "One day."

After running his hands over his face, Jacob leaned forward, elbows on his knees. "I'm sorry," he said. "I can't imagine what that was like."

"Not great," I said. "I keep telling myself that I'm fine, and I am. Most of the time."

Sitting up, he turned to face me. "Are you really?"

I dabbed at my damp cheeks and chuckled. "Like I said, most of the time. This week has been a little rough. My boss is having some health issues and needs me to run the business pretty much by myself. Throw in the dates that, as you know, haven't gone well, and my defenses aren't as strong as they usually are."

Jacob pulled a handkerchief from his back pocket, which might have been the sweetest thing ever, before scooting close enough to dry my face. "You're pretty tough, Meredith Rebecca Witherspoon."

"I'm a crying mess, and the only reason I've physically survived this week is because of you, so I'm not feeling all that tough right now."

He held out the kerchief with a smile that included a hint of dimples. "I'm sorry I was so hard on you yesterday."

I took the offering and shook my head. "Don't apologize. I was wrong for going on those dates if I didn't want to. That wasn't fair to those guys."

Elbow on the back of the bench, he leaned his head against his palm. "Were you serious earlier about wanting to go on this one?"

I suddenly felt like a teenager again, wanting a boy to like me. "I was. You're the first guy whose made me want to try again."

"For the sake of full disclosure, I should tell you my story before we go too far. It might change your mind about me."

"Are you going to cry too?" I asked, trying to lighten the mood. "Because I've made a mess of this handkerchief and I don't think you'll want to use it."

With a tilt of his head, he said, "I'll do my best not to."

"Okay then," I replied. "Tell me your story."

CHAPTER THIRTEEN

Before Jacob could get started, a crew member discovered us and said all passengers needed to be at their tables, so we were escorted to the second level and thankfully shown to a table for two with an excellent view of the city. The meal was served buffet style and since we were seated late, we were welcomed to visit the buffet right away.

Still reeling from the emotions of telling Jacob the truth, and nervous about how the rest of the night would go, I couldn't imagine eating much. At the same time, I'd eaten like a bird all week and suddenly felt ravenous. I stuck with items that wouldn't be too messy to eat and wouldn't leave me needing a breath mint before dessert.

When I returned with my plate, Jacob was already at the table, though he rose and was chivalrous enough to push in my chair as I sat down. Not a common occurrence for me. The truce we'd formed upstairs remained, but now there was a strained awkwardness. At least for me. During our previous encounters, he'd been a stranger that I felt no need to impress. He was just a guy—granted, a very kind and attractive one—who gave me a couple of rides and walked with me for a while.

Between our auspicious beginnings, the very raw emotions I'd displayed mere minutes ago, and my lack of dating experience, I was more nervous than I could ever remember being. That should have scared me, since that meant this evening really mattered, but there was an excitement as well. A sense of forward motion I hadn't experienced in far too long. And that wasn't just the boat moving beneath me.

"I guess I should ask what Lindsey told you so I know where to start," Jacob said as I cut into my asparagus.

I tried to recall all the snippets of information she'd shared, which wasn't much. "She said you teach history, so I guess that's your one other job."

He nodded. "That's right."

What else? "She mentioned that you've been in Pittsburgh for eight years, that you have a calm, comforting demeanor, and that you're divorced."

I wasn't sure how he'd feel about her sharing the last part, but if I'd learned anything in the last few days, it was that honesty really was the best policy.

His knife paused mid-cut but otherwise he didn't react. "I'm not sure about the comforting part, but the rest is accurate. My parents emigrated from Korea to the Atlanta area in the early eighties, and that's where I was born and raised until I left town for college, where I met my ex-wife, who was from here. We started our life together close to my parents, but Jill wasn't happy, so we moved to be closer to her family."

That couldn't have been easy. "Can I ask why you didn't move back after the divorce?"

"For one, my parents aren't there anymore. I'm not sure how much you know about the history of South Korea, but life over there is much better now than it was when they left. They went back about five years ago and I make the trip to see them every summer."

"And there's a second reason?" I asked.

He nodded, his eyes on his food. As he cut the steak into smaller pieces, I started to fear he might not want to share the rest, which was fair. He wasn't obligated to tell me anything. But that didn't mean the curiosity wasn't killing me.

"The second reason," he finally said, setting down the knife and fork, "is because my daughter is here."

That I did not see coming. "Your daughter?"

"Yes. She's six and her name is Sophia, but I call her Sophie. She lives with my ex-wife and I have visitation." Elbows on the table, he joined his hands with a sigh. "She's the reason for the three jobs. Making the alimony and child support requires finding other means of income."

The expression on his face spoke volumes. Clearly, other women had reacted poorly to learning this information. Since I hadn't even considered dating in the last two years, I also hadn't thought about the implications and possibilities of finding someone new in my thirties. People had histories. And in many cases, they had children.

"I bet she's beautiful," I said. "Does she get to go with you to Korea?"

His jaw loosened as he visibly relaxed. "Yes, she went with me last year, and I hope to take her again this summer." As if wanting to be sure I was listening, Jacob said, "None of this bothers you?"

A fair question. Maybe I would have a different reaction once I was able to digest the details, but right now I was simply relieved. There were much worse things he could have shared that would have been deal-breakers, but this wasn't one of them.

"I'm sure that dating while being a single dad with a daughter comes with its own complications, but learning that you have a daughter doesn't bother me, no."

"I also basically told you that I don't have a lot of money."

"Who does?" I asked, loading a bite of potatoes onto my fork. "I make a good enough living to afford my apartment and do some flea market shopping now and then, but I also don't have the monthly expenses that come with owning a car or having a family to feed."

Jacob went back to eating. "That isn't the usual response I get."

"Really? Which part puts them off more?" I asked, truly curious. When you find your life partner at age sixteen, you don't have to think about how much life—or debt—the other person brings into the relationship.

"That's a good question, actually. I'm not sure." He chewed his steak while contemplating his answer. "Probably both. Between the jobs and time with Sophie, I haven't given dating much effort either. Most of these reactions were from my attempts shortly after the divorce."

That led to the obvious next question. "Why did you agree to this date then? I got the impression during our encounters that you weren't a blind date enthusiast."

"What gave you that idea?"

"You asked me why I wasn't finding my own dates."

"That was based on the dates your friends were finding. You have to agree they weren't stellar picks."

That was an understatement. "So it's okay to let your friends pick your dates so long as they pick the right ones?"

"I'd think that would go without saying."

And here we were again, having a fun tit-for-tat conversation that made me smile and want for more. Testing the waters, I asked, "Are you glad you came?"

He loaded his fork while flashing a grin that curled my toes. "I am. Are you?"

"Glad that *you* came?" I said, being facetious. "This dress would have been a waste if I was sitting here all alone."

"It's a nice dress," he offered. "That color looks good on you."

"Thank you," I said, making a mental note to thank Megan for choosing it.

Now that we'd gotten past the hard part, I had high hopes for the rest of the night.

I COULD NOT HAVE IMAGINED this date going so well. We finished dinner and relocated once again to the top deck, where the wind whipped my hair right out of the bobby pins. We laughed as we collected them from around my feet. Jacob assured me that I still looked beautiful, which made me blush, and we took a seat to watch the city lights come back into view. The afternoon shower had moved on, taking the clouds with it and leaving the sky clear and filled with stars.

As I saw the dock approaching, I racked my brain for a way to keep the date going. Two and a half hours simply wasn't enough. But we'd eaten and I couldn't think of what else we could do. I wasn't interested in hitting a club. That wasn't my thing, and we'd never be able to talk over the volume of the music anyway. I could always ask him to take me home, but that still meant the date would end far too soon.

To my relief, Jacob solved the dilemma for me.

"Do you want to take a walk up to the shops?" he asked as we stepped off the boat. The man read my mind.

"I'd love that."

The trees lining the walkway back to Station Square Drive were filled with tiny fairy lights and I couldn't help but smile as we passed beneath them. We'd yet to so much as hold hands, and I wasn't sure if I wanted that to change or not. This was still new, and there'd been moments during the cruise when I'd felt... I wasn't even sure what word to use. Guilty? Knowing that I wasn't doing anything wrong didn't silence the irrational thoughts that I was somehow betraying Brian.

Brian wasn't here. But through some twist of fate, I was. There was no reason I shouldn't go on with my life.

"Do you like event planning?" Jacob asked as we made our way past the Sheraton toward the bustling shopping area ahead.

"I do," I replied. "I've always loved list making and organization. Add that every event results in making people happy and there isn't a better job out there."

"I don't know," he said. "I like teaching. Shaping young lives. Expanding the minds of future generations."

"Dodging spitballs and dealing with parents who think their kid can do no wrong," I added.

With a deep chuckle, he nodded. "I forgot your best

friend is a teacher, too. You must plan a lot of weddings. That doesn't bother you, after what happened?"

Excellent question. "I couldn't do them for the first year. My boss was great. She took them all and let me do the non-wedding events. That's why I owe her now. I probably would have quit if she hadn't gone out of her way to make things as easy as possible. Even when I spent three months unable to get out of bed let alone plan anything, she gave me the time I needed."

"She must have understood what you were going through. Did she have a similar experience?"

I hadn't considered the possibility. "Maybe? My boss doesn't share much about her life. She's recently been diagnosed with cancer and she won't even tell me what kind or any of the details. We've worked together for eight years and I probably know more about you than I do about her."

"Some people are more private than others," he pointed out.

"Is that why Lindsey doesn't know you have the other jobs?"

Hands in his pockets, he stared off into the distance as we strolled at a leisurely pace. "There are a few of us who have other jobs, but it isn't something we talk about openly. It's no secret that teachers don't get paid enough in this country. I've lost count of how many colleagues have quit over the years because they move on to other jobs that pay more."

"And probably come with less stress and better hours," I offered.

"That too. How about we talk about something less depressing?"

"I'm all for that. How about a first date version of twenty questions?"

"That sounds slightly less fun than a root canal," he replied, "but I'm game."

I nudged him with my shoulder. "I'll go easy on you, promise."

He cast a challenging glance my way. "So you get to go first?"

"It was my idea," I pointed out.

Jacob nodded toward the sidewalk on our left. "Okay, then. Let's go have a seat by the fountain and I'll let you grill me."

We'd reached the main shopping area where a courtyard sat closer to the water, offering a beautiful view of the city skyline and featured a long, colorful water fountain. We made our way through the crowd and stepped into the courtyard at the same time a small family vacated one of the benches. The wind coming off the water was cooler now, and I shivered as I lowered onto the seat. Seconds later, I found Jacob's jacket draped around my shoulders.

"You'll get cold," I said, trying to refuse the offer.

"I'm never cold," he stated, ignoring my protests.

As his heat and scent surrounded me, I leaned back

and pulled the coat tight beneath my chin. "If you're sure."

"I'm sure. Start your questions."

As our shoulders met, I could feel the tension running through him. What did he think I was going to ask? His political leanings? His social security number? His number of sexual partners? No one should ever ask that last one. Not unless they wanted to start a fight or develop some new insecurities.

"Favorite ice cream?" I said, hoping to put him at ease.

He hesitated before saying, "You can't judge me for this."

"Who judges someone over an ice cream flavor?"

"You'd be surprised. I like mint chocolate chip."

Oh, now I got it. "I love mint chocolate chip. And no, it does not taste like toothpaste."

"Are you just saying that?"

"No, I swear. We can go get some right now. Except I might shiver my teeth out of my skull if we do."

"I wouldn't want you to lose your teeth," he teased. "Next question."

Very considerate of him. "Favorite music?"

He turned and leaned an elbow on the back of the bench, far more relaxed than when we first sat down. "Most anything, but my favorite group is ONE OK ROCK."

What a coincidence. "I saw them in concert like six

years ago," I said. "They're so good."

Dark eyes widened. "You know who they are?"

Offended, I poked him in the chest. He was rock solid and I nearly forgot my next thought. "Yes, I know who they are. Why is that so surprising?"

"You don't look like the Japanese rock music type."

"Don't make assumptions about me, Mr. Kim. I'm much more hip than I look."

Failing to hold in his laughter, he said, "My apologies. You're very hip. Next question."

I rattled off the common ones—favorite movie, favorite food, favorite color—to which he gave quick answers. It was time to turn up the heat.

"Now for the tougher ones," I said. "Cats or dogs?"

"Definitely cats."

"Ding, ding, ding. Right answer. Coffee or tea?"

"Both."

"Feels like a cop-out, but I'll let you slide. Call or text?"

"Call."

We hit our first impasse. "Are you a sociopath?" I asked.

"Is that the next question?"

"No one calls anymore."

"I do. And I'm counting that one. The answer is no, by the way. Next question."

Why did I have to find smart-asses so attractive?

"I'm running out of ideas so one more, and then it's

your turn." I had to make this one count. What did I really want to know? Watching the fountain shoot water toward the sky in long narrow streams, the perfect question came to me. "Why did you come back for me that night I hit the tree?"

"Was I supposed to leave a helpless woman on the ground?"

He was dodging the question. "You showed up too quickly to have only come back because I might be injured. You stopped before I ran into that sycamore, didn't you?"

Rubbing his palms on his thighs, he came clean. "Yes, I did. I told myself not to look back, but you were so cute I couldn't resist."

Heat raced up my neck. "You thought I was cute?"

"I did. You were so determined to get that guy home safe, even though you couldn't possibly have carried him far. I was impressed that you didn't give up."

That wasn't the impression I got. "You kept giving me judgy looks in the mirror," I reminded him. "I thought you found me annoying."

"Judgy looks?" he repeated. "I was trying to figure out why you were with that guy. I was actually relieved when you said he wasn't your boyfriend."

Now he was just messing with me. "Relieved?"

Jacob stretched an arm along the back of the bench and twirled a lock of my hair. "Yeah. I hadn't even considered dating for more than a year, but I found myself wanting to know everything about this beautiful, capable woman who landed in my car. Which is why I left in such a hurry."

My brain was starting to short-circuit. I wanted to lean into him and at the same time I wanted to leap off the bench and run. This was what I'd wanted, but then why did it feel so wrong? The sounds of the river and the crowd around us grew louder in my ears until I couldn't concentrate on anything Jacob was saying.

Sensing the panic about to take over, I bolted to my feet. "I should get going."

"I didn't get to ask my questions yet," he said, rising to stand with me. "Are you okay?"

"I'm really cold."

Looking around, he said, "Do you want to step into one of the stores to get warm?"

What I wanted was to go home. "I'll be fine once we're moving."

Looking confused, as he should, Jacob ran a hand through his hair. "Okay, then. Let's walk."

When we reached the street, I turned left, knowing the quickest option to get away was to ride the incline back up to Mount Washington. I could easily walk home from there. Instead of the comfortable pace we'd traveled before, I turned on my downtown power walk, which wasn't easy in those shoes.

"Becca, did I do something?"

"No," I said far too quickly. "It's just late and I have

to be up early in the morning," I lied.

"I can drive you home then." He stopped to turn around. "My car is in the garage down by the boat dock."

I turned to walk backwards but didn't stop. "You go ahead. I'm going to take the incline."

"Wait." I was practically running by the time he caught me. "Becca, what's going on? I thought we were having a good time."

How did I explain that I couldn't stop thinking about my dead fiancé? That I was about to have a full-on breakdown in the middle of the street over a man I should have let go of a long time ago? There was no rational explanation for what I was feeling, and knowing that made the panic even worse. This man had seen me flat on my back on the dirty ground, embarrassed and covered in alcohol, and passed out in a crowded restaurant.

He would not see me crumble into pieces on a city sidewalk.

"Jacob," I said, holding up a hand when he reached for me. "I'm sorry. I thought I could do this. I *wanted* to do this. But I can't."

"You can't what? We're just taking a walk."

"There's more than taking a walk going on here. I like you, but I really need to go home."

Concern etched in his features, he held up his hands in surrender. "Just let me take you home. You don't have to talk. I won't ask any questions. Just let me give you a ride."

"I don't need a ride." Pointing to the station a half block away, I said, "There's the incline right there. I ride it all the time. I'll be fine."

"You don't look fine. I can't let you walk away like this."

"Yes, you can," I snapped. "I'm sorry. Please. I'll be fine. Just let me go."

That was two lies in a matter of minutes. I was really racking them up.

"Text me when you get home," he said. It was an order not a request.

"I will." I didn't want him to worry, or worse, come looking for me if I didn't. He knew where I lived, after all.

"At least call someone else. Someone who can stay on the phone with you while you walk home."

A reasonable idea, but I wasn't kidding when I said I did this all the time. I'd probably made this same trek a couple hundred nights before.

"I'll call Josie when I get to the top." Realizing I was still wearing his coat, I slipped the soft material off my shoulders and handed it over. "Thank you and I'm sorry."

"Stop saying you're sorry. You haven't done anything wrong."

But I did. I shouldn't have gone on this date any more than I should have gone on the others. Even if I wanted to this time. Without another word, I took one last look at him and then walked away.

CHAPTER FOURTEEN

I MANAGED TO MAKE THE TEN-MINUTE WALK HOME FROM the incline station without shedding a tear. Maybe I'd shed my quota in the last two years and there were none left. I didn't call Josie, as I said I would, but as far as lies went, that was low on my list for the night.

At the top was going out with a perfectly wonderful man when I had no business doing so. At least this time I couldn't claim peer pressure. No, I'd gone on this one willingly. Excitedly even. But part of me knew that nothing had changed. That I hadn't changed.

I did send the promised text to say I was home. I owed Jacob that much. He'd written back saying that I could call if I needed anything. Without responding, I silenced my phone and tossed it onto the coffee table. I didn't need that kind of temptation.

Bundled up in my bunny pajamas, fluffy robe, and a

pair of winter socks, I stretched out on the couch under a blanket and after nearly thirty minutes, finally started to feel warm again. Milo slept on my stomach, purring in peaceful contentment.

"I'm such a mess, buddy," I murmured, stroking a hand along his soft fur. "Thank you for loving me anyway."

Closing my eyes, I tried to shut out everything that happened in the last few hours, but all I could see was Jacob's face. Smiling as we collected flying bobby pins. Confused when I changed so abruptly. Concerned as I practically ran away from him. I clearly didn't deserve a guy like him, and he definitely didn't deserve me and my baggage.

I sank lower into the couch and pulled the blanket up under my chin, which shifted Milo onto my chest. He continued to purr. Tomorrow was my last day before the real chaos of Amanda's hiatus would begin. I planned to sleep in, eat lots of comfort food, and not speak to a single, solitary soul.

The combination of exhaustion and Milo's purring quieted my thoughts and I felt myself easing into sleep when someone started pounding on my front door like the building was on fire. Heart racing, I heard Josie yelling, "Becca, open up!"

Sliding to the door in my fluffy socks, I unhooked the chain and flipped the deadbolt before swinging it open. "What's that matter?"

"Oh, my God," she said, enveloping me in a bear hug. "You're all right."

"Why wouldn't I be all right?" I asked, struggling to speak with my neck in a virtual choke hold.

Josie pulled back, her hands grasped tightly on my shoulders. "Why aren't you answering your phone?"

Could I not get one night of peace? They didn't need to know every detail of the date within minutes of it ending.

"I put it on silent. What's going on? Is someone hurt?"

"We thought you were!" Blond ponytail swinging, she went from concerned to angry in half a second. "Jacob called Lindsey and said you were upset at the end of the date and he was worried about you. When you didn't answer her texts or calls, she sent me to check on you."

Now *I* was angry. "I'm not a child who needs to be checked on. Maybe I didn't answer because I wanted to be left alone. Did anyone think of that? I just want to be *alone*."

"I'm sorry but when someone tells me my best friend, whose gone through some serious shit over the last two years, acts weird and then doesn't answer her phone, I get worried. Forgive the hell out of me."

I stormed back to my couch. "I've been a lot of things since Brian was killed, Josie, but suicidal isn't one of them."

"How would I know that?" she said, charging in

behind me. "You don't talk to me. You don't talk to any of us. You say we don't bring him up, but you're the one who wants to pretend that it's in the past and you're fine now. Becca, you aren't fine."

"So I'm not fine!" I screamed, spinning and throwing my hands in the air. "The man I was going to spend the rest of my life with was gunned down in cold blood for no reason the day before our wedding. I am entitled to not be fine after that."

"Yes, you are. So let yourself be *not fine*, Becks. Stop pretending that you aren't still hurting, and let us help you through it."

Emotions I'd been suppressing for months bubbled over, releasing the tears I'd thought were done. "Isn't that what this week was about, Josie? You guys helping me *move on* by sending me out on these stupid dates. Even when I told you over and over again that I didn't want to go out with anyone. Damn it, I shouldn't have to let another man into my life in order for you four to leave me alone."

"Becca, we—"

"Just go back to your apartment and tell Lindsey that she doesn't need to worry. I'm not doing anything stupid."

"I—"

"Close the door on your way out," I snapped.

Shoulders dropping, she shook her head and said,

"We love you, Becks. We just want you to be happy again."

My friends needed to face reality. "I'm not sure that's ever going to happen. And if I'm all right with that, then you guys have to be too."

Josie opened her mouth to argue, and then closed it again. Hugging her own bathrobe tight across her chest, she said, "I'm sorry."

Two words I was ridiculously tired of hearing. I nodded and silently stood my ground until I heard the door click shut behind her. Then I folded to my knees, face pressed against my palms, and cried myself to sleep on my living room floor.

A WEEK LATER, I stood in the warm sun in front of a house I hadn't walked into since the week I lost Brian. As I'd predicted, the first five days without Amanda in the office had been unbelievably busy, but I'd welcomed the constant distraction. When I was working, I didn't have to think about the past week or the past two years. All of my focus was on the clients, and there wasn't time for anything else.

My friends gave me the space I needed. There'd been a few text messages in which they'd attempted to check in without actually asking how I was. I didn't ignore them, but I didn't send long replies either, and no one brought up the confrontation between me and Josie.

I felt bad about that, but I didn't regret finally saying what I should have told them long before now. I was sorry that it came out the way it did and that Josie had to bear the brunt of it, but the words needed to be said. My life would be different from now on, and they needed to accept that just like I did.

Jacob sent a text on Sunday. I owed him an apology, which should have been done in person, but there was no way I could have handled that. I retyped the text three times until I felt confident I'd expressed remorse while also making the finality of our connection clear. There would be no more oddly fateful run-ins. And no more dates.

I was doing him a favor by letting him off this train wreck before we left the station.

On Thursday, I'd found a free hour in my afternoon and the thought of sitting quietly with the voices in my head drove me to make an unplanned phone call. My old therapist, Roberta, had miraculously been between patients and was able to talk. After listening to my summation of the last couple of weeks, and the truth about how I'd been struggling even before that, she suggested two things.

One was to come back to see her, and I agreed that would be a good idea. The other was to visit the one person who understood my loss as much as I did. Maybe even more so. And that was how I got here, in front of the house where Brian grew up.

This wasn't a surprise visit. I would never do that to Maggie. She'd been like a second mom to me, and I should have taken the time to see her more often, but running from the memories had meant running from her as well.

The running stopped today. With sweaty palms and a nervous stomach, I climbed the stairs to the Finnegans' front door. Not much had changed. Where my parents' house was a dark-red brick, the Finnegan home was a light-tan color, but the same general shape—a boxy three-story with a rectangular covered porch that spanned the width of the house. This was pretty much the blueprint for houses all over the city.

For nearly half my life, I would have walked in without knocking, but that wasn't the case anymore. With one last deep breath for courage, I tapped on the glass storm door three times. A dog immediately started barking and I took two steps back. The Finnegans didn't own a dog the last time I was here.

An excited white boxer charged into the foyer and pranced from right to left while barking loud enough to be heard three blocks away. He—or she—didn't look vicious, but I wasn't going inside without some assurance of the fact. Mac Finnegan appeared seconds later and offered a familiar smile through the glass.

The large man who'd always been quick with a smile

looked to have aged ten years in the two since I'd seen him. The reddish-brown hair was a little thinner. The green eyes slightly dimmed. The lines of age a little deeper and more obvious.

"Yes, Penny, I see her," he said loud enough for the dog to hear him. She quieted immediately but continued to prance as if she was about to get a very big treat. "She's harmless but we haven't broken her of the jumping yet," he said as he opened the door while keeping one hand on her collar. "Come on in."

As I stepped inside, Maggie joined us in the foyer. "Mac, take Penelope out back, will you?"

Someone meeting her for the first time would immediately think that Maggie Finnegan looked young for her age. The dark hair bore no streaks of gray. The skin around her eyes was still fresh and nearly wrinkle free. But I could see the change right away. Maggie's true glow had always come from the inside. That glow wasn't there today.

"I can do that," her husband said, "but not before I get a hug from this one." The older man who'd welcomed me into his family the moment his son introduced fifteen-year-old me as the girl of his dreams wrapped an arm around my shoulders and squeezed tightly before pulling back. "It's been far too long, my girl. We missed you."

Struggling to hold it together, I said, "I missed you, too."

Mac then dropped a kiss on Maggie's cheek before

disappearing into the kitchen with the dog in tow. We stood in silence, two women who had lost the same person, hovering several feet apart but forever linked together.

"I'm glad you called," she said and motioned for me to follow her. "I made that tea you always liked and some soda bread cookies. You like those, too, don't you?"

The scent of the cookies hit me the moment we entered the kitchen. "I do. I haven't had them in forever." Or since Brian's wake, but there was no need to be that specific.

"Have a seat at the table and I'll bring everything over."

I pulled out a heavy oak chair and lowered onto the bright-green seat cushion before sliding a hand along the polished surface of the table. How many nights had we played games here, with Brian and his younger sister Jenny bickering over who had cheated first? Then there'd been the countless holiday meals when the adults had gathered in the dining room and us teens, which included four of their cousins, had opted to sit together in here.

They'd still called it the kiddie table, and none of us cared so long as we didn't have to listen to boring conversations about politics or how the world was going to hell in a hand basket. When Jenny—the youngest of the group—entered her twenties, we finally renamed it the big kids' table.

"Here we go." Maggie set a tray on the table that

included two mugs and a plate of cookies. She set a white mug covered in four-leaf clovers in front of me. "I put in a splash of milk like always."

The like always hit me hard. I could pretend that not a day had passed since we last sat together like this. Since I'd drank her tea and eaten her cookies and chatted with her around this table. We could talk about the weather and the summer ahead and what she was going to plant in her garden this year, but that wasn't why I was here.

"Thank you. I really appreciate you making time like this."

"Honey, there's no making time," she said, placing her hand over mine. "We're always here for you. How have you been?"

Filling my lungs, I said, "Not great, actually." It felt good *not* to say I was fine. "I know I should be better by now, but all that time heals stuff isn't proving to be true for me."

"I understand that more than you know."

That she suffered too would always break my heart, but that she understood how I felt meant everything. Maggie was the only person, other than Roberta, who didn't offer platitudes or tell me that everything was going to be okay.

"Two years is a long time," I said. "I wasn't sure if you'd want to see me."

"Oh, Becca, why would you even wonder? You were like a daughter to us."

I was, but they lost their son because of me.

"That day…" I started. The tears began and I had to clear my throat to continue. "I was supposed to pick up his tux. If I'd gone like I was supposed to, Brian wouldn't have been in the mall. He wouldn't be—"

"Nonsense," she said. "Do you think this would be better if it had been you instead of Brian?" Maggie left her seat to kneel in front of me. "Becca, the only person to blame for my son's death is that lunatic with a gun. Losing you would have ripped Brian apart. You're stronger than he ever was. We have never blamed you for that day, and we never will. My God, honey, is that why you stayed away?"

"It should have been me. We had so much to do that day, and if I'd stuck to my schedule, then I'd have picked up the tux and Brian wouldn't have been anywhere near there." I bent over to press my head against my knees. "He would still be here with you."

Maggie pulled me to the floor where I sobbed into her shoulder. I hadn't even realized how much I needed her forgiveness until that moment. I would have given anything to change the past. To have been the one in the line of fire. Maybe I'd have gotten there earlier and missed the whole thing. Maybe I'd have been victim number one. Either way, Brian wouldn't have had to die.

"Listen to me," she said, pushing me away to cup my face in her hands. "We will never know why that man went into that mall to kill people. We will never know why Brian had to be in the wrong place at the wrong time. But I know with all of my heart that he loved you more than life itself, and if he had known that going there would save you, he'd have done it. He'd have walked in there without a second thought."

"But he didn't know," I whispered.

"Neither did you, baby. How could you? No one knew. But I have never once blamed you." Maggie brushed the tears from my cheeks. "You made my boy happy. You gave him joy while he was here. That means everything to me. I can never thank you enough for loving him like you did."

Breathing through the hiccups, I said, "I miss him so much."

"Me, too. But I missed you as well. Please don't stay away anymore."

I nodded as I dried my eyes. "I'm sorry. For everything."

She pressed her lips to my forehead. "There's nothing to be sorry for. I'm just glad to have you here. Now, how about we go out back so I can show you the garden and you can meet Penelope where she's less likely to jump and break something. She's going to love you."

"I would like that."

We got off the floor together and after going through several tissues to dry my eyes and blow my nose, we took our tea and cookies outside where I met the sweetest dog who gave the most enthusiastic kisses I'd ever received.

There was no magic pill that would fix my broken heart, and the guilt I felt didn't magically disappear. But Roberta had been right. Healing required dealing with the hard stuff.

Today was really hard. And cathartic. And to my surprise, an enormous relief.

CHAPTER FIFTEEN

ANOTHER WEEK PASSED AND I WAS STARTING TO GET A grip on handling all of the active events we had going. Not having to deal with new clients turned out to be a blessing, though it still concerned me. We would eventually run out of business or have to take on jobs with very short notice in order to keep money coming in. Neither outcome was appealing, but I had to believe Amanda knew what she was doing. She was a shrewd businesswoman and I couldn't imagine her making a decision without considering every possible angle.

She'd surprised Marquette and I by showing up Wednesday morning unannounced. Wearing jeans and a Guns & Roses T-shirt—a look I had never seen her in before—she stayed long enough to get an update on how things were going, and then she left again. I couldn't tell if she'd lost weight or the jeans were just way too big for her normal size, but her face was definitely paler, and the dark circles beneath her eyes were new.

"Do you think she's all right?" Marquette had asked.

I truly didn't have an answer. Frail was not a word I associated with my boss, but if a six-foot-tall woman could appear fragile, that's how I'd describe her.

"Cancer treatment isn't easy for anyone, but I'm sure she'll bounce back." I had no less than three aunts who had gone through breast cancer and come out the other side to live long, healthy lives. Surely Amanda would do the same. "Let's just keep this place going so she can focus on herself."

Between Friday evening and Saturday night, I had three events back-to-back so I was relieved to be on my couch with a book in my hands and a feline curled up against my side on Sunday morning. The reprieve didn't last long before someone knocked on my door. No one had called to say they were coming over, so I had to assume it was Mrs. Zhang looking for her cat again. Ling Ling liked to roam the building and often stopped by for a treat and a visit with Milo.

To my surprise, I found Lindsey on the other side of the door. "What are you doing here?" I asked.

"I'm taking you out," she said, strolling past me. "Get some clothes on."

I didn't want to go out. I didn't want to see people. I just wanted to sit in my quiet apartment. Alone.

"Linds, I don't feel like—"

"This is an order, not a request." She crossed to the couch, snagged a magazine off the coffee table, and sat back. "I'll wait while you change."

My best friend had always been bossy, but I wasn't in the mood to humor her today. "I don't want to go to lunch."

"I don't remember asking what you want." Her eyes remained on the magazine. "You can change or you can go like that. The choice is yours."

Considering my options, I remained near the door, longing to shove her out and slam it behind her. But I knew that would be pointless. I also knew she'd drag me out of here in my panda pajamas without a second thought.

"Where are we going?"

"You'll see."

"I need to know what to wear."

Her eyes finally shifted my way, her expression one I knew all too well. She was annoyed. Well, so was I.

"I'm not taking you to the symphony, Becca. Just throw on some jeans and a T-shirt already."

My newfound ability to say no went only so far. I could get her to leave, but I might say something I'd regret in the process. Did I want her out of my house? Yes. Did I want her out of my life? No.

"Fine. Give me five minutes."

"You get two."

What the hell? “I haven’t even brushed my hair yet today.”

Closing the magazine, she tossed it back on the coffee table. “No one is going to see you where we’re going.” That sounded like something a killer would say after pulling you inside a rusty old van. “The clock is ticking,” she added with a sinister smile.

Yeah, that wasn’t creepy at all. Without another word, I charged into my room, changed like a firefighter who just got the call, and in an act of defiance, took an extra thirty seconds to run a brush through my hair. I needed a shower and made a note to clean up my eyebrows before bed, but otherwise felt presentable enough for whatever deserted location she had in mind.

Ten minutes later, Lindsey took the Carnegie exit off the Parkway and I assumed we were going to clean out her classroom. There was still technically a week of school left, but that was for exams so no actual teaching took place. We did this every year, but we’d never done it on a Sunday before.

When she veered right instead of left after the underpass, I knew my assumption was wrong.

“Where are we going?” She’d said there would be no one around so that ruled out lunch at one of our regular spots. Neither of us had spoken up to that point, and Lindsey remained silent. “Stop being so cryptic and tell me where we’re going.”

“We’re going to visit someone.”

"You said no one would see me. Did you lie just to get me in this car?"

Lindsey shook her head as she took a left at the light. "I didn't lie. Chill out. We're almost there."

Once we drove over the creek and onto Carothers, I knew where she was taking me. And I was furious.

"You cannot be serious."

She once again remained silent.

"Don't do this, Linds. I won't get out of the car."

"That's up to you."

"Take me back home."

"Nope."

"Then drop me at my parents' house. Drop me on a freaking corner, for all I care. Just let me out of this car." As we made the right onto Magazine Street, I started to beg. "Lindsey, I can't do this today. Please, don't make me do this."

Ignoring my pleas, she made the left past the church and I stared at my hands to keep from seeing the rows of stones spread out like soldiers ready for inspection. I hated it here. And I hated her in that moment. The car rolled on, down the narrow lane that led to the newer section of the cemetery. When she pulled off and cut the engine, I closed my eyes and gripped the seat belt as the lifeline that would keep me in this seat.

She couldn't make me get out. Not unless she planned to drag me kicking and screaming. Lindsey undid her own seat belt and left the car. Seconds later, my door opened and I quickly closed it again, then locked it.

"Really?" I heard her say through the window a moment before the lock clicked and she opened the door again. "It's called remote keyless entry, Becca. Are you really going to stay in there like a petulant child?"

"I told you I wasn't getting out."

"Why not? Isn't this where you want to be?"

How could she be so cruel? "You know damn well I didn't want to come here."

"But you might as well, since you've decided that your life is over. We might as well dig a hole right now, right next to Brian, and then you can be happy."

Furious, I turned to get out and strangled myself with the seat belt. More annoyed than embarrassed, I extricated myself from the vehicle and pushed her backwards. "I told Josie and I'll tell you. I'm not going to kill myself."

"Of course not," she said, unfazed. "That would be too easy. You'd rather punish yourself for the next fifty years."

Pacing away, I shoved my hands through my hair and when I looked up, I realized I'd walked straight toward his grave. Without turning around, I said, "It's my fault he's here."

"Then it's mine, too. After all, you couldn't pick up his tux that day because *my* car broke down on the way. Remember that part?" Lindsey came up behind me and spun me around. "Should I be punished, too, then? Should I dig a hole for myself right beside yours?"

"Stop it," I said. "I had options. I could have left you waiting for the tow truck and gotten a ride. I could have called my mom or his mom or Josie or Megan or Donna and had that tux picked up. It was my job. It was on my list of things to do."

"And you had no fucking idea that a madman would walk into that mall hours later and start shooting people. You left out another option. The one where you could ask Brian to pick up his own goddamn tux, which he should have done in the first place, and that's the one you chose." Throwing her hands up, she grunted in frustration. "Becca, you didn't send him to his death. You sent him to the mall. Stop blaming yourself for something you had no control over."

She made it sound so easy. "You don't understand what I'm going through."

"I don't understand?" she screamed. "Becca, he was one of my best friends. We were the three musketeers, remember? We spent nearly half of our lives together, and I may not have been the woman he was going to marry, but I loved him like a brother. I watched you go through hell for months, and it killed me that I couldn't take that pain away. So don't tell me what I do and don't *understand*."

I'd been so busy drowning in my own misery, I hadn't bothered to consider how she felt. One of Roberta's favorite sayings came back to me, and for the first time I understood what she meant.

"Grieving is a selfish endeavor," I said, quoting the words aloud. "I'm sorry that I couldn't be there for you, Lindsey. I'm sorry that I didn't see how hard it was for you. But I don't know how to let this go. Why do I get to go on with my life when he didn't? Am I supposed to find someone else and be happy and pretend he never existed?"

Using her sleeve, she dried my cheeks. "Becca, moving forward doesn't mean leaving him behind. Brian was the most alive person I ever met. He attacked life like every moment deserved to be celebrated, and never took a day for granted. You know he'd want us to do the same. And he'd want *you* to be happy. That's how we keep him alive, hon. That's how we not only remember him, but we honor who he was."

I turned to look at his tombstone. "He *would* be pissed to see the way I've been acting," I said with a chuckle. "There are days when I'd swear he's with me, Linds. Now I realize he's probably been shouting at me. Giving me pep talks and pushing me to keep going. To not give up."

"I can totally hear him doing that." Putting her arm around my shoulders, she pressed her head to mine. "No one is asking you to forget him. We just want you to remember that you're still here."

Squeezing her hand on my shoulder, I said, "I'll work on it."

JUNE ROLLED in like the freight train I knew it would be. Between the graduation parties and a slew of weddings, my weekends were booked solid. Amanda had been out for nearly a month, but had let us know that she'd be returning to the office two days a week, which meant Marquette had to go back to playing receptionist. I'd only survived the last few weeks because we'd made the executive decision to ignore Amanda's mandate.

Normally, Marquette would answer the phones and take messages, which I would then return to answer the client's questions. This seemed completely pointless when he had as much access to the files as I did, and half the time knew the answer without having to look it up. He handled the setup crew scheduling. He made sure vendors knew where to be and when to be there. When it came to logistics, I might as well have been the middleman, so skipping me entirely made sense.

So long as we didn't give any of Amanda's clients a reason to complain, she would never be the wiser, and I could keep my sanity. Since she'd announced Monday and Wednesday as her days in the office, we weren't left guessing on when she might make a surprise appearance again. The only problem was that this week, I needed

Thursday afternoon off, and needed her to cover a meeting I couldn't change.

How that would go over I didn't know, but I'd agreed to help Lindsey clean out her classroom and to attempt to talk to Jacob while I was there. That meant putting on my big girl panties and making the request.

"Can I talk to you a second?" I asked, approaching her as she dove into her mid-morning Hershey bar. This was a new habit and I would not begrudge a cancer patient her daily dose of chocolate.

"What is it?" she said, nodding toward the chair at the corner of her desk. The color had returned to her cheeks, and though she'd lost weight and wore wigs to cover her now bald head, she no longer looked as frail as she had at the beginning.

I took a seat. "It's about Thursday. I can't cover the Fleming meeting."

She stopped typing. "Why not?"

"I have something I need to do that afternoon."

"Reschedule your something."

A month ago I'd have done exactly that, but not today. "I can't do that, and we can't move the meeting either. The Flemings are driving in that morning, and only staying long enough to tour the venue. You'll have to meet with them."

Amanda leaned back and crossed her arms. "Last time I checked, I was the boss here, and I'm saying you can't have the afternoon off."

With a white-knuckle grip on my coffee mug, I scooted forward in my chair. "I've been running this business by myself for weeks. You won't bring in anyone else, and you won't let Marquette take on more responsibility. I understand that you're going through something right now, but, Amanda, I never ask you for anything. I show up. Always. I don't think one afternoon is too much to ask."

Her jaw twitched as she stared at me with narrowed eyes and for half a second I thought she might actually fire me on the spot. But whether she liked it or not, she needed me. Even if she wasn't going through cancer, she couldn't afford to let me go. I busted my ass for this place, and a huge amount of our new business came from recommendations made by *my* clients.

Returning to her typing, she said, "Fine."

That's what I thought. "Thank you."

She didn't respond and I returned to my desk feeling like a super woman. Roberta had given me a homework assignment to find small ways to put myself first. I felt pretty certain I would be getting an A at our next session.

CHAPTER SIXTEEN

THE DAY I'D MET JACOB ON THE BOAT HAD BEEN stressful and nerve-racking and had nothing on this nondescript Thursday afternoon. As in the past, I was at my old high school to help a friend break down her classroom. Sporting a bright-green visitor sticker on my faded Pirates T-shirt, I did my part—packing workbooks into plastic totes, removing pictures of Emily Dickinson, Charlotte Bronte, and Alice Walker from the pegboard, and sanitizing desks that had probably been in use since I'd been a student.

All while trying to muster the courage to visit the history teacher at the far end of the hall.

Lindsey and I had debated whether or not she should tell him I was coming. Or ask if he wanted to see me. Both felt like too much pressure. I'd decided to wait until the day and if I had the courage, I'd walk down to his room. Courage turned out to have nothing to do with it. Knowing he was so close had me wired and I couldn't imagine *not* going to see him. That may have been why I'd pushed Lindsey to rush through the cleanup so I could do exactly that.

None of this meant I felt confident about how Jacob would react to seeing me. He'd made no effort to contact me since the day after the date, and Lindsey said he hadn't asked about me beyond checking that Monday to make sure I was okay. A word that meant something new to me these days. Dad was right when he'd said there was nothing wrong with *not* being okay, but what Roberta taught me was that struggling didn't make me flawed.

It made me human. Amazing how much better your outlook gets when you accept that.

"I can't fit anything else in this tote," I said, wiping my hands on the back of my jeans. "Do you have another one?"

"Look in the metal cabinet in the back," Lindsey replied. "How much more is there?"

I counted the copies of *The Great Gatsby*. "Fifteen of these and twelve of *Ethan Frome*."

She carried a box from her desk to the counter where I was working. "There's room in here for those."

We packed the books away, and then Lindsey wrote a description of the contents on the side. Clicking the cap back onto the marker, she looked around. "Is that everything?"

"Unless you have more crap hidden somewhere."

That earned me a smack on the arm. "This isn't crap," she growled. "This is what I need to educate future generations."

"What you're doing is boring them to tears." Every book I'd packed up today was dark, dreary, and always had someone die at the end. Most often whatever female character dared to have an opinion of her own. "Why can't you teach something newer? Something not depressing or problematic?"

"Because I have to teach the classics, and classics are depressing and problematic."

"These kids should get to read a love story. A real one. Not that *Romeo and Juliet* or *Wuthering Heights* stuff where no one gets to be happy."

Lindsey carried the newly packed box over to the others already stacked in the corner. "Feel free to come to the next meeting and make that suggestion to the school board. Now," she said, pushing her hair out of her face, "speaking of love stories, don't you have someone to go see?"

Butterflies fluttered to life in my stomach. "Be honest with me. Do you really think this is a good idea?"

She crossed the distance between us and brushed something off my face before examining me from several angles. "Now I do, yes."

I patted my cheeks. "What was that?"

"Just a smudge of dirt. I don't see any more."

Glancing down, I spotted a line of dirt across my thighs. "Why didn't I think of this? Linds, I'm a mess. My jeans are dirty. There's dirt on my face."

"Not anymore," she cut in.

"Seriously, how can I go see him looking like this?"

She waved the question away. "You look adorable, as always. Just go say hello and ask him what he's doing for the rest of his life. It's that simple."

When did my best friend become such a comedian? "What if he says not spending it with you?"

Lindsey shrugged. "Then you say have a nice life and go about your business. Either way, you can't not give this a shot. You like him, right?"

"I do."

"Then go for it. I need to use the bathroom, and then I'll hang out here until you're done. If he suggests you two go out for drinks or something, just text me and I'll know not to wait."

That was not happening when I looked like this. "If we go out again, it won't be while I'm wearing nine months worth of English classroom funk, thank you."

"You need to be more spontaneous," she argued.

"And you need to start worrying about your own love life. Don't think I haven't noticed that all of you are so far up in my business while ignoring your own empty dance cards."

Nose scrunched, she asked, "Who says dance cards these days?"

"Roberta would call that deflecting. You need to find your own Jacob."

"I don't date teachers."

Lindsey had made this baseless declaration before. "That will always be weird, and you know that isn't what I meant."

"There's nothing weird about it. I want to be able to vent about my day to my significant other without having some competition over who has the worst students or who has the most papers to grade."

Pointing out the obvious, I said, "Why not just find someone who wouldn't see it as a competition?"

"I'll put that on my boyfriend order form. Now go before he leaves and you miss him."

Shaking my hands to cool my suddenly sweaty palms, I took a deep breath. "I can do this. I'm just saying hello, right? How hard can that be?"

"Not hard at all. Especially when you know the guy already likes you." Lindsey shoved me into the hall. "Room 105, down there on the left."

Staring past the empty metal lockers, I nodded as if accepting a dangerous mission. "I'm ready."

She gave me another gentle push. "Go get him, tiger." When I gave her a what the hell look, she added, "I don't know where that came from. Just go."

As Lindsey headed off in the other direction, I made my way down the hall with my heart beating in my ears. What was the worst that could happen? He could tell me to go to hell. Or slam the classroom door in my face. Both of those I could survive. They would suck, but I'd survive.

Shoulders back, I picked up my pace while reminding myself to breathe.

TWO DOORS away from Room 105 my cell phone rang. I'd promised Marquette that I would be on call so I checked the screen to find the name of a local hospital. Why would a hospital be calling me?

Tucking into the alcove of a closed door, I answered. "Hello?"

"Hello, I'm calling from the University of Pittsburgh Medical Center downtown. Is this Becca Witherspoon?"

My heart rate kicked up a notch. "Yes, it is."

"Ma'am, I have you down as the emergency contact for a Ms. Amanda Crawford. She came in unconscious through our emergency room a few minutes ago."

Since when was I Amanda's emergency contact? "What happened? Is she all right?"

"The doctors are with her now, but we don't have a lot to go on. Is there any way you could come to the hospital?"

Stuttering, I said, "Yes, yes, of course, I can. I… I'm in Carnegie right now but I'll get there as soon as I can." I panicked at the idea of having to wait for a car, then remembered I was with Lindsey. I needed to find her. "Is she going to be okay?"

"I'm sorry. I have no other information right now."

"Right." I stepped out of the alcove to go in search of Lindsey and realized they probably didn't know about Amanda's condition. "She's going through cancer treatments right now. Could that have anything to do with this?"

"What kind of cancer?" the woman asked.

Feeling like the worst person ever, I said, "I don't know."

A moment of silence came down the line before the woman said, "You're her emergency contact but you don't know what kind of cancer she has?"

I did not need this stranger questioning my relationship with my boss. "I work for her," I said, as if that cleared up everything. "I'm with a friend so as soon as I find her, we'll be on our way."

I ended the call and started to jog down the hall, trying to remember where the bathrooms were, when Jacob rounded the corner.

"Becca?"

Too freaked out to stop and explain, I said, "I'm sorry. I can't do this right now."

"Do what?" he said, blinking in confusion. "Why are you here?"

"I was helping Lindsey but I have to go. I'm sorry."

Another twenty yards down the hall I found the bathroom and sprinted inside. "Linds? Are you in here?"

"Becca?" came a voice from the second stall down.

"I just got a call from UPMC. Amanda's in the emergency room, and I need to get there."

The toilet flushed a second before she said, "What's wrong with her?"

"I have no idea. They said I'm her emergency contact and they need me to come down there."

The stall door opened and she hurried to the sink. "Since when are you Amanda's emergency contact?"

Another question I couldn't answer. "I don't know, but I'm probably the worst one ever. I couldn't even tell them what kind of cancer she has."

"That's her fault, not yours. The keys are in my purse in the classroom so we have to get that first." She snagged two paper towels from the dispenser. "Did you talk to Jacob?"

Impatient, I shifted from foot to foot. "The phone rang before I got there but I saw him in the hall on my way here. I told him I couldn't do this right now."

"Did you tell him why?" she asked, her eyes wide.

The memory of me sprinting away from our date while saying *I can't do this* flashed through my mind. "Oh, no. I was too panicked about Amanda. He's going to think it's the date all over again."

Grabbing my hand, she dragged me out of the bathroom. "We have to find him."

"Lindsey, there's no time. I have to get to the hospital."

"Then we'll yell it through his door on the way by." She stopped long enough to snatch her purse from her desk and we were off again. At Jacob's classroom, we burst inside only to find the room empty. "Shit," Lindsey mumbled. "Where is he?"

There was no time for this. "I'll have to explain later. We need to go."

Looking around for I had no idea what, she ran over to the chalkboard and wrote *Call Lindsey* in big letters. "That should do it," she said. "Let's go."

We took the hallways at a full run as I sent up a string of silent prayers that Amanda would be all right.

THE DRIVE to the hospital seemed to take forever and for once I didn't mind Lindsey's aggressive driving. How she didn't get a ticket was nothing short of a miracle. Hopefully, there would be more of those today and Amanda would be all right.

"I'm Becca Witherspoon," I said as I rushed to the desk directly inside the emergency room doors. "I got a call that my boss is here. Her name is Amanda Crawford. Who do I need to talk to? Can I see her?"

The woman behind the desk offered a calming smile.

"I'll let them know you're here. Have a seat and someone will come out and get you."

"Thank you," I said, but didn't bother taking a seat. Instead, I paced the area, which was nearly empty. A man and a young boy occupied two chairs on the far side. The boy stared at a phone, while the man twisted his baseball cap over and over in his hands.

I had a fresh understanding of how he must have felt and added another prayer to my own that whoever he was here for also made it through.

"She's going to be okay," Lindsey assured me. "Amanda is tough, right? Maybe she just had a dizzy spell."

"Dizzy spells don't land you unconscious in the emergency room," I pointed out.

"Miss Witherspoon?"

I spun to find the source of the voice. "That's me."

"I'm Dr. Patel. Can you come with me, please?" said the heavyset woman wearing a white doctor's coat over her blue scrubs. "Your friend will need to stay here."

"I'm good," Lindsey said, nodding for me to go along. "I'll be here when you come back."

I followed the woman and once we passed through the large double doors, she said, "Ms. Crawford is awake and alert. You telling us that she's going through cancer treatments helped us discover the issue."

I didn't feel particularly helpful considering I couldn't give them any other information. "What was it?"

"The treatments made her anemic. Many of the symptoms she was experiencing are the same as a heart attack so that's where we were going until we heard from you. Then we ran a test and thankfully found the simpler answer." She pushed through a large tan door. "Ms. Crawford, your friend is here."

I'd never called Amanda my friend before. After eight years of working together, I should have. We might not hang out on the weekends, but we spent a great deal of time together and though a bit private—or excessively private—she was still a good boss and a good person. The fear of losing her had been real, and not because I feared for my job security.

"Hey, Becca," Amanda said. She was lying on a gurney with a long tube coming out of her left arm. "Sorry if I freaked you out."

Not what I expected her first words to be.

"Are you okay?" I asked.

"I've been better."

Dr. Patel patted her on the leg. "She's going to be fine so long as she keeps an eye on how she's feeling and doesn't ignore any other episodes in the future."

"No one likes a snitch, Doc."

"This has happened before?" I asked, feeling like the most horrible person ever for making her take that meeting so that I could talk to a man. Such a stupid reason to send my boss to the hospital.

"According to Ms. Crawford," the doctor said, "she's

been having dizzy spells for a couple of weeks but didn't mention them to her oncologist."

Amanda held up her hands. "Dizziness is a side effect of chemo. I thought it was normal."

"Now you know that yours is a sign of something more serious." Glancing my way, the doctor said, "We're going to keep her overnight to make sure the transfusion does its job, but you can take her home tomorrow."

"She can't take me anywhere," Amanda said. "Becca doesn't drive."

"I can still get you home," I defended. "Thank you, Doctor. I appreciate you taking care of her. I'll make sure she doesn't ignore anything else."

As the doctor left the room, Amanda stared at me with brows arched high. "You're my keeper now?"

"You obviously aren't doing a very good job of keeping yourself." I fluffed her pillows. "Why didn't you tell me that you made me your emergency contact?"

The high and mighty expression faded as her gaze shifted to her feet. "I didn't think there would be any emergencies. I had to pick someone, and you're the only person I could think of."

Not the most feel-good explanation ever. "I might have been more helpful if I had more information," I reminded her. "They asked me what kind of cancer you have and I couldn't tell them. It's your right not to share the details, but—"

"It's ovarian," she cut in. "Stage three. They plan to take all of the parts, but I have to do the chemo first."

At nearly fifty, I had to assume there were no plans for her to have children now, but that didn't mean a full hysterectomy would be as easy as having a tooth pulled. When Mom had her hysterectomy four years ago due to cysts, she'd struggled with the idea of losing her womanhood, as she'd put it at the time. Once she'd recovered and was relieved of the constant pain, she hadn't given her "womanhood" a second thought.

"How do you feel about that?" I asked, fully expecting to get a vague answer. Or no answer at all.

"It sucks. Not that I had any plans to have kids. I knew years ago that would never happen." She straightened the blanket across her stomach. "I guess I just thought I'd go out with all the parts I came in with, you know?"

A valid reaction. "Can I ask how you knew you'd never have kids?"

She sighed. "I suppose it's time I tell you that story. Have a seat. This will take a minute."

Shocked that I was about to learn something so personal about my boss, I grabbed the chair from the corner of the small room and dragged it to her bedside. "I'm ready to listen."

CHAPTER SEVENTEEN

"I THINK I MIGHT HAVE MENTIONED A FIANCÉ TO YOU once, right?"

Hovering on the edge of my seat, I said, "You did, but then you told me I'd imagined it or that I must have heard you wrong."

She shook her head. "You didn't. I met Luke when I was sixteen and fell head over heels. He was a couple years older than I was and came from a rough family that didn't have much. My mom *hated* him." With a smile, she leaned her head back. "That made me want him even more, of course. We ran away together when I turned eighteen, and had two glorious years before he decided the only way we could really be happy was to go back and do things the right way. Luke was determined to win my mother's approval."

"He sounds like he really cared about you," I said,

afraid of where this was going. If this man broke her heart…

"Yeah, he loved me," she said with a wistful sigh. "I was content the way things were, but you couldn't stop Luke once he got an idea in his head. The stupid man went and joined the military in the middle of a freaking war. He figured we'd be apart for a few years, but once he got home he could go to college on the government's dime, and then we could start our life together with my family's blessing."

Something told me that didn't happen. "I think I know where this is going."

"It isn't hard to figure out from there," she said. "He got shipped to the front line, and I never saw him again."

My heart broke for her and I realized Jacob had been right that her compassion when I lost Brian came out of personal experience.

"I'm so sorry."

Amanda ran a hand through her short blond hair and stared up at the ceiling. "You're probably the only person I know who understands what that feels like. Our stories aren't exactly the same, but close enough."

She was right. I knew how if felt to have your future ripped away. I also knew the frustration of being offered platitudes about how everything happens for a reason, and loving once is better than never loving at all. People could shove those cliches right up their collective asses.

"Did your family come around before he died?"

Shaking her head, she said, "That's the really messed-up part. Mom had the nerve to tell me that I was better off without that loser to bring me down. I walked out of her house that day and never spoke to her again."

So she lost more than just the man she loved. "No one should have to go through all that."

As if snapping out of a trance, she sat up straighter on the bed. "Well, that's my sad story. Let me be your cautionary tale, my dear. Don't let one tragedy ruin the rest of your life. I've been wallowing in misery nearly as long as you've been alive, and all I did was rob myself of having a family of my own." Tapping the mattress, she added, "And now cancer is going to take the parts I never used anyway. No big deal, right?"

A tear rolled down her cheek and I knew she didn't want or need an answer. Rising from the chair, I said, "I'm going to hug you now. Is that okay?"

At first she looked at me as if I'd suggested we make out, but then she nodded as the crying started in earnest. I wrapped my arms around her shoulders, careful not to crimp the tube going into her arm. Incredible that we could have so much in common and yet I had no idea. Not that she'd been all that open, but there must have been signs I missed. Moments of commiseration or a look in her eye that would have given me a clue.

At least I'd seen Brian the morning it happened. At least our families loved each other and we'd gotten so many more years than Amanda and her Luke did. Life really did suck a lot of the time.

Once the crying ebbed, she pulled back and wiped her eyes. "Are there tissues around here anywhere?"

I glanced around and found a box on the small counter beside the sink. "Here you go."

After blowing her nose and drying her cheeks, Amanda took a deep breath. "I didn't mean to dump all of that on you."

"Dump away. That's what emergency contacts are for, right?" Saying the words brought a question to mind. "How exactly did they know that I'm your emergency contact if you were unconscious when you got here?"

She pointed to the cell phone beside her leg. "That's how you're listed in my phone contacts. My oncologist said to make sure I had someone in there. I don't know who called for the ambulance, since I passed out while standing beside my car, but they told me the guy found the phone next to me with my email open. He made sure the screen didn't go off so that whoever needed info from it could get into it."

I doubted I'd have thought of that. "Wow, that guy might have saved your life."

"That's a bit dramatic, Becca, but I *am* lucky he was there." Rubbing the area around the needle sticking out of her arm, she said, "Didn't you have something to do this afternoon? Did I mess that up?"

Now it was my turn to confess.

"I was going to talk to a guy that I went out with a couple of weeks ago," I said. "The date didn't end well, and I was hoping to get a second chance. This is more important though. I never should have made you take that meeting for something so ridiculous."

"There's no need to apologize. I'm just happy you're dating. I've been worried about you."

I had never once gotten the impression my boss was worried about me. "Really?"

"It's the reason I came back to work earlier than I planned. I was going to surprise you, but since Marquette knows, I'm sure you'll know soon enough." Amanda crossed her arms before remembering the needle. With a mumbled expletive, she put her arms back at her sides. "I've put out an ad for two new planners. Marquette is already getting resumes and submitted his own. Some look promising. I shouldn't have put all of that work on you when I took off, but I needed to keep things as simple as possible while dealing with the treatments. There was no way I could go through the hiring process at the same time."

"You're hiring *two planners*?" I said, unsure how much more new information I could take in one today. "That's… great. Does this mean we're going to open to new business again?"

She nodded. "Once we get the June weddings out of the way, we'll open back up." The next words out of her mouth might have been the most shocking of the day.

"I'm sorry, Becca. I know I'm a shit boss a lot of the time, but I appreciate you sticking with me. I'll do better in the future." After a brief pause, she said, "I'll try anyway."

Before I could respond, a nurse stepped into the room. "Ms. Crawford, it's time to take you upstairs." Crossing to the machine with the empty red bag hanging at the top, she added, "And it looks like perfect timing. Let me get you unhooked, and then we'll get you moved."

Remembering that my ride was still here, I said, "I need to tell Lindsey that I'm going upstairs with you. She drove me here and is waiting in the lobby."

"You're fine," Amanda said. "You go and I'll message you tomorrow when they're ready to let me out of here."

"Are you sure? I can stay."

"There's no need for both of us to be bored all night. You go find that guy you went out with so I can live vicariously through you in my old, ovary-less age."

The nurse laughed as I said, "You aren't old, Amanda."

"Don't argue with your boss," she replied. "Now go."

I cast the nurse a concerned look and she said, "We'll take good care of her, hon. No need to worry."

Clearly outvoted, I conceded. "All right, I'll go then. Call me if you need me before tomorrow."

Amanda waved with her free hand while the nurse worked on the needle in her arm. Getting that out was not going to be fun and I made my exit before any blood appeared. On my way back to the lobby, I tried to process all that I'd just learned, and had the bold idea to convince my boss that there was still time for her to find love. After all, you never knew who was going to drop into your life when you least expected.

A fact I knew all too well.

"How is she?" Lindsey asked when I found her in the lobby.

"Good," I said. "The cancer treatments have caused anemia, but she didn't know because the symptoms are the same as the regular chemo side effects. They gave her some blood and are keeping her overnight, but I need to come back tomorrow to get her. Would you—"

"Say no more," she cut in. "We'll get her home for sure. Are you okay, though?"

An odd question. "I'm fine, why?"

Lindsey tilted her head as she stared at me with narrowed eyes. "You're smiling, but not like your normal smile. What's that about?"

I wasn't sure how much to share. Amanda had taken eight years and one medical scare to tell me about her past. She probably wouldn't appreciate me sharing the details with other people. There was one development I could talk about.

"Amanda says she's going to hire two new planners, and she apologized for expecting me to do all of the work while she was out."

Eyes wide, Lindsey leaned back in surprise. "Are you serious right now? Your boss? Amanda Crawford? The one who barks at you like a drill sergeant and has never thanked you for anything? That woman apologized to you?"

Some of that was true, but I felt bad about making her sound like such a monster. "She's been good to me overall. When Brian died, she was probably the best boss I could have had. I doubt anyone else would have given me the time and space I needed the way she did." Now I knew why that had been the case. "I guess facing down a deadly disease softens a person. Whatever the reason, my life is about to get easier. Or at least my job is."

"Becca, that's fantastic. And long overdue."

"Can you just be nice about it for now? Amanda isn't perfect, but there are much worse bosses out there." We made our way toward the hospital doors. "Do we need to go back to the school?"

"I'll take care of the rest."

"I'm with you so I might as well help."

Lindsey shook her head. "No, you go on home."

She said this as if I would get in my own car and go. "Are you not going to drive me?"

When we reached the sidewalk outside, she stepped in

front of me and turned her back to the parking lot. "I've got things to do so I ordered you a car."

What the…? "What do you mean you ordered me a car? Just take me home."

"I can't do that."

This was starting to get weird. "What's going on? Why do you look like you just swiped a cookie or something?"

With an arched brow, she silently stepped aside. That's when I saw him, looking as sexy as ever, leaning on the white Buick, arms and ankles crossed.

"What did you do?" I whispered, unable to take my eyes off of him.

"Like I said. I got you a ride."

The implications in that second sentence sent heat rising up my cheeks. "I'm not ready for this, Linds."

Giving me a push to get me moving, she said, "You're beyond ready, hon. I told him what happened back at the school. Coming here was his idea."

My heart threatened to leap out of my chest. "Are you serious?"

"Yes. Now go. And remember that you deserve this."

I really wanted to believe that.

"I'll call you tomorrow," I said.

With each step I took, my body felt lighter and lighter until I was afraid I might float right over him. Jacob didn't move. He just waited. As I got closer, his beautiful lips curled into a grin and the stark beauty of him made me dizzy.

"Hi," I said.

"Hi," he replied.

"What are you doing here?"

"I came to see you."

"Why?" I couldn't believe I asked such a stupid question, but my brain screaming *throw yourself at him* was making it difficult to think.

Jacob lifted off the car and tucked a loose lock behind my ear. "Lindsey said you were upset about your boss. I wanted to make sure you were okay."

"I am," I nodded. "And so is my boss. Mostly. I mean, she has cancer, which has given her anemia—or the treatments have actually—so she's not totally fine but she's fine right now." Oh my God, I was babbling. This was not good. "Um… are you okay? I'm sorry about what happened back at the school. And that night at Station Square. I—"

"Becca," he said, cutting me off.

"Yes?"

"Do you want to get a pizza with me?"

I opened my mouth and then closed it again. Of course, I wanted to get a pizza with him. I loved pizza. But I was a mess.

"You mean right now?"

"Unless you have something else to do, but it looks like your ride is leaving, so…"

"I just…" Looking down at my dirty jeans, I said, "I'm not really dressed to go out."

"You look great to me, but we can always pick it up and go somewhere else to eat it. Somewhere that we can talk."

Feeling like the luckiest woman alive, I accepted the offer. "I'd like that a lot." Then an idea struck. "Actually, I know a place."

Jacob laughed and I'd never heard anything sweeter. "Did you just say I know a place?"

Now he had me flustered. "Don't laugh at me. I mean it literally. There's a courtyard at my building that no one ever uses. We can eat there."

Brow arched, he said, "So you're inviting me back to your place?"

"To my building," I corrected. "That's it. For now."

Looking off into the distance as if considering the offer, Jacob looked back down and said, "I can live with that. For now."

This man could give flirting lessons and I was not a worthy opponent. "Then I'm going to get in the car."

His deep chuckle paired with those dimples was going to be the death of me. "That's a good idea. But first…" Jacob leaned down to place a quick kiss on my lips before saying, "You're really cute, you know that?"

I didn't feel cute. I felt warm and dizzy and a dozen other things, but cute was not one of them.

"I'm a little rusty at this," I said. "And you're really good at it."

With a tap on my chin, he said, "You'll get better."

ON THE WAY to my place, I called to order ahead from Joe Cestone's Pizzeria and we swung by to pick it up. At first, Jacob had said whatever I wanted was good with him, until he heard me add mushrooms as a topping. Then he suddenly had an opinion, and I agreed to only order mushrooms on half.

"You need to pull into the main parking lot up ahead," I directed when we approached the building. "The courtyard is on that side."

He did as asked and minutes later we were seated at a small round table with our giant slices of pizza and lots of napkins. The breeze carried the scent of rose bushes, and the sounds of smooth jazz drifted down from an open window on the second floor.

Not sure how to begin, I asked, "Did you get everything done at school?"

"I did." Jacob took another bite before wiping his mouth. "This is really good."

"Cestone's is my favorite."

We fell back into silence and I started to worry. What if we had nothing else to talk about? What if he thought I was boring? He'd only seen me constantly going out on dates. The poor man had no idea how dull my life truly was.

"You owe me," he said, dragging me from my thoughts.

"I'm sorry, what?"

"You owe me," Jacob repeated. "I answered your questions on our date, but I never got to ask you anything."

That was true. My early and embarrassing departure had robbed him of his turn. "Fair is fair," I said. "Fire away." To my surprise, he pulled a slip of paper from his pocket. "What is that?"

"I'm a teacher. I never present a quiz unprepared."

"A quiz?" I repeated. "Am I going to be graded?"

Anchoring the paper with the corner of the pizza box, he said, "This is more of an entry assessment."

That sounded worse than a quiz. "What happens if I fail?" I asked, half serious. I didn't really think he'd get up and leave if I gave an answer he didn't like, but the way my luck had gone lately, nothing would surprise me.

Leaning close, he said, "Then you'll have to spend extra time with the teacher."

Well, that didn't seem like too bad of a punishment. "All right then. Start the assessment."

Jacob checked his notes. "We'll start with an easy one. What's the number one item on your bucket list?"

That was easy. "To visit Asia."

"You didn't even have to think about it," he said, a hint of shock in his tone.

I took a bite and then dropped the slice back onto the open box lid, which I was using as a plate. "I've wanted to visit Asia since I was a little girl. My grandmother was a flight attendant back when they were still called stewardesses, and she had this amazing collection of pictures she'd taken from all over the world. Her favorite destinations were places like Singapore, Tokyo, and Taiwan." Remembering the hours I spent listening to her stories made me smile. "She made them sound beautiful and romantic and fascinating. I know they're all different today than when she was there, but I still want to go."

"I haven't been to the other two," he said, "but I've visited Tokyo and I agree that it's all of those things."

"Really? How many places have you been?"

Jacob shook his head. "We'll get to that later. Right now, I get to ask the questions."

Properly chastised, I sat up straighter. "Yes, sir. Next question then."

He consulted his list once again. "If your apartment was on fire, what's the one thing you would grab before running out?"

Again, I didn't have to think about my answer. "Milo."

"Your cat?"

"Yes, my cat. Who wouldn't save their cat?"

"I didn't say anything," he replied. "Just most people say their phone or their laptop."

Heartless people, maybe. "Those can both be replaced. I couldn't replace Milo."

"You couldn't find another cat?"

"I didn't say that. I said I couldn't find another *Milo*." Jacob pulled a pen from his back pocket and wrote something on his list of questions. "What was that?" I asked.

"I'm giving you bonus points for that one."

He really knew what to say to make a girl swoon. "That's very sweet of you."

Clicking the pen, he read the next question. "How would you describe your dream date?"

Two answers came to mind, but I needed a little clarification. "Date as in the person or the activity?"

"The activity."

"Oh, that's another easy one."

Clicking the pen again as if ready to take notes, he said, "I'm listening." I waited until he looked at me. "Well?"

"This," I said. "This is how I would describe my perfect date."

Crossing his arms on the table, Jacob leaned forward. "You're an easy woman to please, then."

"If you think getting here was easy, you haven't been paying attention."

His laughter surrounded me, and I knew I would never get tired of that sound.

Jacob reached down and tugged my chair across the pavement until my knees slid in between his. "I'm glad you didn't give up before our date."

My mouth went dry as his voice dropped an octave, and I could feel his warm breath on my cheek. "I'm glad you were the one on that boat."

His eyes dropped to my lips. "I'd really like to kiss you right now."

Breathless, I whispered, "I really wish you would."

When our lips met, his hot and soft and gentle against mine, there was no panic or doubt or urge to run away. I slid my hands into his thick hair and leaned in for more, amazed that anything could feel so perfect.

When we drew apart, he pressed his forehead to mine. "I want to keep seeing you, Becca."

Impatient for more kissing, I murmured, "Yes. Definitely, yes."

EPILOGUE

Like most places around the United States, Pittsburgh offered an epic fireworks display every Fourth of July, and the best place to watch the show was from the Mt. Washington overlook. A quick ten-minute walk from my apartment and I had the best view in the city, provided I didn't mind squeezing in with a few thousand other onlookers.

My proximity to the action meant that all of my friends gathered at my place in the evening after spending most of the day with their families. This year, we had two extra guests.

"We need to start walking that way in about fifteen minutes," I said, while Josie and Lindsey finished stuffing leftovers into my fridge. Their mothers insisted that they take home enough food for an army, and for some reason, most of it always ended up at my place.

It was as if they feared my lack of cooking skills would result in total starvation, which was ridiculous when I had cold cereal and could order in whenever I got hungry. At least this year I had someone to help me eat it all.

"Be easy with him, honey," Jacob told Sophie, who was being overly affectionate with Milo. Since I'd adopted him as a full-grown cat shortly after losing Brian, I had no idea if the furball had ever been around children. Thankfully, he showed immense patience with Sophie despite her exuberant hugs.

"She's okay," I said. "I think he likes the attention."

"I don't want her to hurt him," he replied. "I know how much that cat means to you."

After nearly a month of dating, I still pinched myself that this dear, caring man had fallen into my life. We'd survived the busy month of weddings, mostly due to Jacob not minding weeknight dates and not having to rush home for work in the mornings.

This was my second time meeting Sophie, and I was pretty sure she only liked me because of Milo. Apparently, her mother was not a pet person. If her adoration of my cat was any indication, her father would have a kitten by the end of the summer.

"Hey, Sophie," Megan said. "Do you like to read books?"

"I do," she said in her cute little voice. Truly, everything about the child was adorable, and she had the calmest nature. I had a good hunch where she got that from.

"Well, I have some in my bag. Do you want to check them out?"

I may have given Megan a heads-up that Sophie would be joining us. I didn't exactly keep toys around my apartment, and I'd been afraid she'd get bored.

"Sure," she said, shoving Milo onto the floor as she slid off the couch. Reaching Megan, she leaned on the arm of her chair and asked, "What do you have?"

The librarian pulled three books out of her bag. "Have you read any of these?"

Clapping with excitement, the child pointed to the last one. "I love this one. Can I read it now?"

"We have to leave soon," Jacob reminded her.

With big brown eyes that matched her father's, she looked up with a protruding bottom lip. "I can read until we go, can't I, Daddy?"

Crumbling immediately, he said, "Okay, honey."

The poor man didn't stand a chance. I could only imagine what lay ahead in his future, and I grinned thinking about watching her wrap him even tighter around her finger. It was cute now, but in another ten years he would be pulling his hair out in frustration.

And I would still be enjoying the show. Hopefully.

As Sophie carried the book back to the couch, Josie sat down on the floor by the window. "Meg, are you going to play softball again this year?"

"You play softball?" Jacob asked.

"Don't look so surprised," she replied.

All of my friends had taken to Jacob as soon as they'd met him, and he'd developed a quick rapport with each of them. He and Josie picked at each other. Donna, who had yet to arrive, had taken to calling him hot stuff, which made him blush every time. And Megan had won him over with her love of history. The pair had spent nearly an hour the first night they met discussing everything from the Revolutionary War to the Geneva Peace Accords.

"Megan shakes off her quiet librarian persona once she hits the field," I explained. "She can throw a mean line drive to first base, and pitchers hate her because they can't find her strike zone."

"An added benefit of being short," Megan added.

She and I high-fived, united in our petiteness.

"What team this time?" Lindsey asked, joining us with a handful of corn chips.

"It's a new coed team. We don't start until September so I don't know the whole roster yet, but I've heard a few familiar names tossed around. Unfortunately, Fletcher is one of them."

Us girls collectively growled, and Jacob said, "We don't like Fletcher?"

"He's her ex," Lindsey said around the chip in her mouth. "After three years, he told her she was boring and dumped her for his secretary."

"Lindsey," I snapped.

"What? He asked."

"It's okay," Megan said. "All of that is true."

"He sounds like a real jerk," Jacob said.

"He is," Josie confirmed. "He'll be laughing out his ass when that secretary figures out what a piece of crap he is."

"We must be talking about Fletcher," Donna said as she strolled in with more leftovers.

"How did she know that?" Jacob whispered. I kissed him on the cheek and said, "You'll get used to it." To Donna, I said, "You cannot put any more food in my fridge. I already have too much."

"Okay. I mean, if you don't want Mom's potato salad…"

I leaped off my chair and grabbed the bag dangling from her hand. "I can make room." After doing just that, I checked the clock. "Donna, you're just in time. We need to head out if we're going find a spot where the little one can see, too."

Megan went straight to Sophie and offered a hand. "You want to walk with me?"

"Sure," the little girl said.

I set my chin on Jacob's shoulder. "You'd never know she runs the children's program at the library, would you?"

"I'd never have guessed."

The group headed out, with Megan and Sophie leading the way, Donna, Josie, and Lindsey in the middle, and Jacob and I pulling up the rear. A block from my building, he placed a kiss on the back of my hand and said, "Have I told you how pretty you look today?"

"Not in the last hour," I replied.

Nodding toward the crowd in front of us, he said, "I think Sophie is having a good time."

We'd spent the day with my parents, who'd doted on her from the minute we walked in. Mom was practically giddy for the last week since I'd told her we were bringing Jacob's daughter. She'd even gone out and bought games and puzzles and a kit to make slime so that Sophie would have plenty to do. Though I was pretty sure most of the purchases had been an excuse for her to practice her grandma skills.

When I'd told her about Jacob and that he had a little girl, I'd thought she might pass out from excitement. Not just because of the potential ready-made grandchild, but because it was obvious how happy I was.

And I *was* happy. Blissfully so.

"I'm surprised she hasn't passed out yet," I said. The Finnegans had stopped by my parent's house with Penelope, who had been even more excited than Mom at this new tiny playmate. The pair had run around the backyard until I was exhausted just from watching them.

"I'll have to carry her back after the fireworks," Jacob said. "I can already tell that she's running on fumes."

Tucking in close to his side, I said, "I'm really glad you got to bring her today. She's so sweet."

"Thanks for letting me. I wasn't sure how you'd feel about it."

I tugged on his hand. "Jacob, she's welcome anytime. I told you before, you having a daughter doesn't scare me off. I mean, it's early and I'm still nervous around her, but she's part of you, and that's all that matters."

Dropping his voice so the others couldn't hear, he said, "Is there anything that *would* scare you off?"

"Is this another test?" I asked.

"Not a test. Just a question."

Leaning my head against his shoulder, I squeezed his hand. "I don't think so."

"What if I said I love you?"

Jerking my head up, I met his eyes. "You love me?"

He nodded. "Yeah, I think I do."

Unable to contain my smile, I said, "I think I might love you, too. Are we crazy?"

"Probably," he said, lifting me off the ground in a tight hug. "But it's the best kind of crazy."

I heard Sophie say, "What are they doing back there?"

"They're just excited for the fireworks," Lindsey said, earning a laugh from the rest of the group.

Jacob put me back on my feet, but I was pretty sure I would not be touching the ground for the rest of the night. Or for the rest of my life.

THANK you for reading Not You Again. I hope you enjoyed Becca and Jacob's story as much as I enjoyed writing it. An honest review is always appreciated!

If you'd like to read the next book in the series coming out later this summer, pre-order Not Playing Fair now and see if Megan finds her own happy ending on the softball field.

Lastly, if you'd like to keep up with me and my books, you're always welcome to subscribe to my newsletter. You'll get a free short story just for signing up. And if you turn the page here, you'll see the full list of my other books.

Thank you again and happy reading!

Terri

ALSO BY TERRI OSBURN

Find them all here

Anchor Island Series

Meant To Be

Up To The Challenge

Home To Stay

More To Give

In Over Her Head

Christmas On Anchor Island*

*coming Oct 2021

Ardent Springs Series

His First And Last

Our Now And Forever

My One And Only

Her Hopes And Dreams

The Last In Love

Shooting Stars Series

Rising Star

Falling Star

Wishing On A Star

Among The Stars

Stand-Alones

Ask Me To Stay

Wrecked

Awakening Anna

ACKNOWLEDGMENTS

I first have to say thank you to the two Kims in my life. To Kim Law for all the brainstorming and plotting and laughter that kept me sane over the last year. And to Kimberly Dawn for being my trusty copyeditor with the endless patience to fix my same mistakes over and over again. I'd say that one day I'll get them right, but we both know that's unlikely.

I'd also like to thank my family back in Pittsburgh for answering the most random questions at the most random times. I lived in the burgh back in the early 90s, and as expected, much has changed since then. At the same time, much has stayed the same. I hope I captured the personality of the city and look forward to spotlighting it even more as the series goes along.

Now to the readers who have stuck by me and been patient while I dug myself out of a mental hole. A year without releasing a book is a very long time, but you jumped right back in when I finally put another one out and I cannot thank you enough for your support and for your kindness toward my work.

You brighten my life daily and I can never thank you enough for that. Much love and happy reading!

ABOUT THE AUTHOR

Terri Osburn writes contemporary romance with heart, hope, and lots of humor. After landing on the bestseller lists with her Anchor Island Series, she moved on to the Ardent Springs series, which earned her a Book Buyers Best award in 2016. Terri's work has been translated into five languages, and sold more than 1.5 million copies worldwide. She resides in middle Tennessee with four frisky felines and two high-maintenance terrier mixes.

Learn more about this author on her website or check out her Facebook page.

Made in the USA
Columbia, SC
28 April 2023